Enthusiastic reviews for Lior Samson's novels –

Bashert (The Homeland Connection)

"Perfect! . . . a page turner that spins a good story."
— *Peter Gordon, publisher*

"Samson writes with a crisp elegance like John Le Carré and weaves his plot magically, sustaining suspense throughout the novel. The ending is a satisfying and surprising climax."
— *James A. Anderson, author*

"An ambitious novel, . . . moving with the speed of light between interconnected events, three continents, and a group of unique and memorable characters. I recommend it."
— *Avraham Azrieli, author*

"Samson keeps the pages turning in this retro-techno-thriller."
— *Brett James, author, film producer*

The Dome (The Homeland Connection)

"Suspenseful and timely, . . . I cannot say enough good things about this novel."   — *Alan Caruba, critic, BookViews*

"An excellent read, and very highly recommended."
— *Midwest Book Review*

"Crisp, sardonic, sometimes amusing, and highly entertaining. [Samson is] a real story teller."   — *James A. Anderson, author*

"Showcases his talent for melding thought-provoking intrigue with non-stop action."   — *Peter Gordon, publisher*

Web Games (The Homeland Connection)

"This extraordinary author has the ability to anticipate events in ways that enhance his novels, and *Web Games*, his latest, is no exception. . . . You will not put it down."
— *Alan Caruba, critic, BookViews*

"An outstanding tech thriller—better than Tom Clancy. . . . This ranks up there as one of the best [thrillers] I've read in 2011."
– James A. Anderson, author

"For readers who want their brain to be well-fed while enjoying the thrill-ride of action suspense. . . . I couldn't put this book down." *– Dawn Jones, teacher*

"The story swiftly pulls the reader into a stream of events, . . . [and] the characters instantly come to life, as if you've known them for years." *– Jos P. van Leeuwen, university professor*

Chipset *(The Homeland Connection)*

"Lior Samson hits another one out of the park. . . . Few thriller writers can match Samson's ability to deliver a gripping story."
– James A. Anderson, author

"Few novelists can match Lior Samson's ability to deliver a multi-dimensional thriller that will satisfy discriminating readers who crave realistic stories populated by flesh-and-blood characters." *– Avraham Azrieli, author*

The Rosen Singularity

"The plotting is ingenious and the characters come through strongly. It succeeds marvelously on the thriller level, but it also delivers a substantial intellectual and emotional kick."
– Rebecca Goldstein, MacArthur Fellow, author

"Vibrant and distinctive characters, and thoughtful, yet engaging narratives and conversations, . . . an exciting, pulse-pounding story." *– Laurie Jenkins, book blogger*

The Four-Color Puzzle

Also by Lior Samson, from Gesher Press

The Homeland Connection:

Bashert

The Dome

Web Games

Chipeset

Also:

The Rosen Singularity

Avalanche Warning

Requisite Variety: Collected Short Fiction

Available from Amazon.com and other booksellers.

The Four-Color Puzzle
Falling Off the Map

a novel by Lior Samson

GESHER PRESS

Gesher Press is an imprint of Ampersand Press
Rowley, Massachusetts

Gesher Press | Ampersand Press
58 Kathleen Circle
Rowley, MA 01969
Author site: www.liorsamson.com

Printed in the United States of America.
5 4 3 2 1

ISBN 978-0-9885275-3-9

Cover and book design: Larry Constantine.

Body set in Gentium, Gentium Book, and Arial, title and chapter titles in Optane Extra Bold, folios and running heads in Optima.

To the memory of Emmet Larkin,
an exceptional teacher whose blunt honesty
kick-started my career as a writer

Experience teaches only the teachable.
–Aldous Huxley

preface

THIS IS NOT THE STORY you think it is. It is not even the story I thought it was.

With this novel, I am writing off the map, well outside the boundaries of my own comfort zone. For my readers who know me as the author of technology-tinged thrillers, this will, I hope, take them in new directions, as it has for me. This excursion has meant digging into the workings of the law and legal procedure and recruiting the help of friends and colleagues in the legal professions. I want to particularly thank Pete Morin, a lawyer and mystery writer of note, who gave me early feedback on legal drama and rich responses to the final manuscript. I am also grateful to Patricia O'Sullivan, another author whose work I admire, for her careful reading and generous feedback. A special shout-out goes to my forensically enlightened friends Elaine Byrne and Phil Samson, whose thoughts helped shape the final product.

And, as always, I am in deep debt to my editor, Janet Lemnah, for her usual professional polish in helping complete this work. To Lucy, my ever-faithful first and final reader, once more I owe far more than can be expressed here. That she takes the time and attention to read and respond to my writing even when it diverts to a new trail, is a gift.

part one: induction

one

SHE HAD SURPRISED HIM, this student with the onyx eyebrow stud and the black lipstick and the raccoon eyes. Suddenly, his view was blocked, blacked out as her crepe skirt brushed the tile floor in front of him. Brad glanced up from the lecture table to her hair: black, not a natural black, shoe-polish black. He looked back down, sorting the quiz papers, concentrating, picking the word. "Impossible."

"Don't say that, Professor Williams." She chewed on her lip. Glossy. Goth. "It's too late for me to drop the course, and I just failed the quiz."

"How do you know that? I haven't even marked them yet. You might have done better than you think." Brad neatened the stack of papers a second time and slid them into his scuffed and battered tan briefcase with the latch that no longer closed properly.

She waited as he finished and as the other remaining student in the seminar closed her iPad and left the room. "I know I failed because I only did half the problems. I ran out of time."

"It was a take-home quiz; you've had since Tuesday."

Of the eight students in MTH 342 Topics in Topology and Geometry, only this girl, Sofia something, was struggling. Brad had always to remind himself to think of them as young women. He had once slipped and referred to "a girl in class" when talking with Emile Breitling. Breitling, a pinch-faced professor of philosophy—a real professor, not a contract instructor like Brad—had delivered a smug, extemporaneous lecture on semiotics and social labels, making clear that Brad's inferior vocabulary was not only dated but denoted a diminished social awareness.

"I need help." Sofia used the right words, the words that were like a key in the lock of Brad's psyche. Then she closed the distance between them, putting herself close enough that Brad could smell the sandalwood scent of her freshly washed hair, close enough so she had to tip her head well back to look him in the face, exposing her neck. Too close.

The lecture table gave Brad no place to retreat. "Look, I really—"

"Tutor me." She fixed her eyes on him.

It was the azure irises, flecked with light brown, the left eye slightly darker and distinctively patterned, that held Brad's attention as she waited, unblinking, for his reaction. "I can't. I'm not regular faculty, not on campus. I live over in West Hopeland. In fact, I need to catch my ride right now."

She arched her brows. "I've got a car. I can give you a lift. This was my last class today. I'll take you to Hopeland. Then maybe you can help me understand this non-Euclidian geometry . . . junk."

No! The exclamation echoed in his head as he composed his thoughts. It was such a hackneyed one-act play. Was it really still being staged by students and teachers in twenty-first century America? What was the unspoken agenda? Was there one? A short-cut to a passing grade? His mid-thirties receding hairline and round face traversed by a sparse moustache hardly seemed to him the stuff of a young woman's fantasies.

Whatever the motive or agenda, he, of all people, could take no chances. His protective instincts kicked in: self-protection and the caretaker in him that wanted to protect Sofia from herself. He could not risk what he had salvaged of his life. He lowered his eyes, glancing from side to side, in search of options, seeking words, looking for the best way out. He tried not to notice the black lace top of her blouse, the freckles around her collar bone.

He took a long, calming breath. "You could talk with Professor Herrington. I'll send him an email, tell him you'll be dropping by. He's right here and might be able to do some tutoring."

She bit her lip. "I was hoping . . ."

"I'm sorry. Dirk Herrington can probably give you some help. Give it a try. You'll get this stuff, I'm sure." More relaxed and off the hook for the moment, Brad raised his eyebrows and let his smile widen. "Okay?"

"Okay." She swung her backpack over one shoulder, untangled the dangling white cords, and inserted her earbuds without turning away.

"Good luck, Sofia." He re-latched his briefcase one more time. "See you in class Tuesday." She drifted toward the door, floating through iPod space. "I really need to catch my ride," he said. She was gone.

Jake Collins, with the Campus Patrol, was his ride home on Thursdays, which meant a brisk hike across the Smith College campus, then forty-minutes of forced small talk before being dropped off at Mandy's Muffin and Mug on Main Street in West Hopeland. At Mandy's, the plane of discourse would become more elevated, as the regulars assembled for the Thursday afternoon conclave incongruously known to its members as the Coconut Club. Then it would be dinner alone while Brad graded papers. Later, he would Skype with Angie, the distant love of his life, thus ending the evening with another Thursday-night custom of longstanding. It was the customs, the small rituals of his regularized life, that helped focus his attention.

He was turning off the lights in the seminar room when he noticed the cellphone forgotten on the lecture table. It was his.

two

A SHOT.

Distraction, dangerous distraction was his downfall, always had been.

A whip-crack.

The ice plating the warped next-to-top step snapped, sending a tree of branching fractures spraying from beneath Brad's boot. His mistake was to look down, fascinated.

Dendritic. Fractal.

Momentarily lost in free association, he swung the other boot up to the landing. As his foot slipped off the edge of the step, he went down, askew, banging his bum shoulder, hitting his chin and splitting a lip. His briefcase landed on the partially frozen driveway, popped open, and vomited paper-clipped and stapled quizzes onto the slush of salt, sand, and ice.

It was a replay of scenarios from his childhood. "You never watch where you are going, Bradley," his mother would say. "Be. Here. Now."

"I was. Here. Now. I was watching," he said, answering a dashiki-clad woman from the past who still followed him everywhere and nagged him to pay attention. He painfully pulled himself erect and clung to the handrail where he had stopped his slide half-way down the stairs. He was grateful to be saved from serious injury by his heavy sheepskin coat and thankful that he had not been carrying his laptop. "That is my problem, Mother, always has been. I do watch. And I see." Suddenly aware that he was thinking aloud, addressing a nagging ghost, he looked around.

Across the street, Jenna Bateau was just getting home, shaking her waist-length hair as she exited her Prius and opened the door for her dog. Brad had been told what breed it was, some popular poodle cross, but he was not a dog person, and the name would not stick in his mind. To him it was a yappy windup toy, a pathetic creature that spent its days being ferried and carried from place to place as Jenna made her social-work rounds of area foster homes. She deducted the dog food and vet fees as professional expenses under the specious argument that the stupid creature was a "therapeutic pet," a facilitator in her encounters with abused and abandoned children. Brad was a skeptic but never said a word when she told stories of miraculous moments catalyzed by her brainless dog.

"You okay, Brad? Be careful. You need to watch your step on those stairs. Wouldn't want anything to happen to you." The inquiry, ill-timed admonition, and affectionate finish from across the street were all synthesized emotion, practiced, as if she were addressing a client. Brad found her intensely attractive physically but was repulsed by her mannerisms and her poorly trained dog, from whom she was never separated. He imagined that the dog would accompany her into bed with any man she ever let get that far. After marriage, perhaps. He knew that she regarded him as an unrepentant sinner given to eccentric interests, which seemed to heighten the appeal for her and made him fair game for salvation. Although she sometimes flirted, Brad could not imagine physical attraction toward him played any role on her side of the well-sublimated seduction.

"Yeah, I'm okay," he called out. "Just slipped on the goddamned ice and dropped my test papers." He pressed his lip with the back of a gloved hand as he cautiously made his way down the remaining steps. He bent to gather the papers, shaking the worst of the sand and rock salt off a stack of them before wadding them back into his briefcase. "My landlady never gets around to the ice on my steps."

His landlady, old Mrs. Hathaway, with her house dresses and Bean boots and voice like a hacksaw, never got around to anything. In fact, it was precisely his responsibility under the terms of a lease that enabled him to afford the rent on the second-floor of the house. He could just pay for it out of the pocket change that was left to him after making alimony and childcare payments to Grace. The outside steps to his apartment, the driveway, the sidewalk were his job. I am falling down on the job, he thought, smiling at his own play on words.

Jenna grinned back at him, apparently encouraged by his smile, though it had nothing to do with her. For a social worker, she could be remarkably impervious to what others were communicating. "Not much longer. Spring comes, even to the Berkshires. Even this ..."—she hesitated, swallowing some minor profanity—"this miserable weather will soon be over."

She was a born-again believer who still struggled against the speech habits of the once freer lifestyle that had followed her expulsion from Mount Holyoke for doing drugs on campus. She had gone through a succession of addictions before settling on evangelism as her drug of choice. "Spring is God's gift to the patient," she sang out. The price of her getting her act together was still being paid in installments by her neighbors who put up with her poodle and her public piety. "Nature's resurrection is a perpetual reminder of the greater Resurrection of our Lord and Savior."

If anything, the other way around, Brad thought, a myth recalling a metaphor. He turned his smile into a taut line and waited until the impulse to speak subsided, then turned to climb the steps again, this time keeping his free hand on the wooden rail and his attention on making it to the top. His lip stung and his shoulder ached. He would pay for his fascination with fractals. The lip would heal quickly, but his shoulder would complain for a fortnight, at least.

Inside, door closed, Brad could still see his breath. Mrs. Hathaway kept the thermostat for the whole house turned down, and Brad used his oven and little electric space heater only sparingly, since the gas and electric were on separate meters for the upstairs. In the winter, he heated dinners in the oven to help warm the place; in the summer he used the microwave because there was no air conditioning. Year-round, the dinners were much the same except for the nights that someone at Mandy's asked him to join them for supper at the Mohegan Diner. There he would insist on paying for his own meal or treating his benefactors but would invariably allow himself to be talked into someone else's treat.

The ritual was fairly well established among the small circle of local intellectuals and pseudo-intellectuals who gathered at Mandy's for conversation late afternoons on Thursdays. Only once had some part-timer wondered when it might be Brad's turn to pick up the tab for coffee and pastries. The dapper and adept Armand Richelieu had, on that occasion, elegantly stepped into the breach by dramatically pulling out his smartphone, then flipping through pages on his appointments app and announcing, "Nope. My turn. Definitely." He even twisted the phone around and waved the glowing screen past everyone's face, too fast to read of course, but a convincing gesture, nonetheless.

Brad had been grateful to Armand, not only for the rescue, but for the style and sincerity with which it was executed. Far better than the rest of the Coconut Club, Armand knew the whole story of Brad's slide from Grace and from a nascent Cambridge career into exile in small-town purgatory. Papal reconsiderations aside, Brad knew purgatory was real, and it was here on Earth, in Western Massachusetts. Elsewhere, too, no doubt.

It was Armand who had sat for hours sipping hot cocoa in the winter or a mocha freeze in the summer, waiting, the two of them passing time talking about everything interesting but nothing real, until Brad had finally opened up about his past and Armand had shared his own secrets. With that, nothing more of a personal flavor had been said or needed to be. Soon after, tables at Mandy's began to be pushed together on Thursdays, as the tight dialogue slowly expanded into a loose colloquy. When Gillian Rappaport joined them after a time, identifying herself as another cocoa nut, the Coconut Club was christened with a sobriquet well suited for an assembly often as obsessed with wordplay and deceptive spelling as with the pursuit of Truth and Meaning and Insight spelled with uppercase initials.

Today, Armand was a no-show, Gillian was not yet back from the Caribbean, and the Coconut Club had adjourned almost as soon as it had convened. There was a winter storm on its way, which gave everyone a rationale for an early departure, but the Club was never at its best without Armand, and Armand was with a new boyfriend over in South Hadley for the second week in a row. If the group had been given to gossip or personal disclosure, Armand's absence might have been a good Topic for Today. But the Club was not that kind of a group. It's attention could sink as low as politics, at least until the discussion drifted from politics to Politics with a capital *p* and then to Political Systems and on to Political Theory, with a long, free-association digression into Plato, Platonism, and then to Platonic and not-so-Platonic relations among contemporary politicians. But the dialogue would never dip to touch on personal politics.

If it was not abstract, it was not fair game; if it was not distant, it would not be allowed close to the table. These rules had never been articulated, but they were understood and consistently observed. The Club was the one venue in the small town where one could talk about Reality without being dragged down to anything real, and card-carrying members fiercely protected the perquisites of their participation.

On occasion, outsiders had stood at the edge and made conversation. A few had even pulled up a chair. "Hi. Mind if I join you all?" would be met with a shrug-and-nod version of The Wave circling the tables. That might be followed by several minutes of noncommittal non-conversation about nothing in particular, the kind of exchange that is the very lifeblood of communal life for normal people. The gaps between comments would gradually lengthen until the gathering sat and sipped in silence, and the discomfited interloper finally excused himself. No one had ever attempted to gain entry more than once. To anyone with intact social sensitivity, the price of admission was too high. On the other hand, complete strangers who were unrecognized members of an invisible brotherhood could join without introduction and be instantly embraced.

Brad was a student of pattern, not only in ice and the irises of a student's eyes, but also in life. At the slight distance of his analytical detachment from the world around him, he had noticed that those who did introduce themselves or who asked if it were all right to join in the discussion invariably proved to be misfits, while those who simply plunged into the Debate of the Day with a counter-argument or a provocative question were more likely to be recognized as kith and welcomed into the colloquium.

Of course, it depended on the form and substance of the intrusion. The Club was not simply a group of guys arguing, joined on occasion by Gillian or another of the local brainy women. Men can argue about many things: about the Patriot's new quarterback and the odds in the Superbowl, about politicians and taxes, about women when no woman is present. Club members were not just argumenttative debaters; they were diggers, seekers after something elusive. They were not merely passing time and consuming caffeine and calories, although these were required rituals; they were intellectual raptors, soaring, seeking a stratosphere where the rarified atmosphere strained the oxygen-starved brain into insight, into intellectual orgasm. The aftermath also followed a pattern: long, wordless moments and nuanced nods as everyone pondered the implications of the day's epiphany. The silence was ultimately broken, always in the same way by the same punctuating word—but—and another search for rising thermals would begin.

Some Thursday nights, the group at Mandy's soared into interstellar reaches. Others, like this one, they adjourned without ever exceeding the treetops, leaving Bradley Williams earth-bound, grading quiz papers for the evening and struggling to keep warm in his drafty apartment.

three

IT WAS STILL THERE, the distraction, the intriguing post from the student who went by the inventive handle of "DeTuring." A detour, waiting.

While the oven warmed to 325° for his meal-in-a-box from the supermarket and the microwave nuked his coffee, Brad had awakened his laptop. The browser was still open to the website where he picked up beer money for online tutoring of high school students. The oddball request for help from DeTuring had appeared three days earlier and had now nearly aged out, pushed toward the bottom of the page because no tutor had responded. It was almost certainly a joke. The subject line read "i need help proving the four-color theorem." Interesting. One of those problems that is so easy to understand, straightforward to formulate, and almost impossible to prove. Almost.

The beeping microwave snapped Brad back from his detour into proving the already proven and reminded him that he had real work to do. He emptied his briefcase and did his best to clean off and smooth out the student papers as he spread and reordered them on the kitchen table.

It no longer bothered Brad that he was hired staff, and, in the minds of the Emile Breitlings of the school, only a few notches up from the custodial crew. He no longer found it necessary in conversation to slip in references to his papers in the *Journal of Social System Dynamics* or to name-drop about his colleagues at MIT or Harvard or to mention the book he had co-authored on stochastic modeling. He was one of seven authors on that, but it was still in print, and the Smith library even had a copy, thanks to a special request from one of his enthusiastic students.

It was for that, the energy and enthusiasm of students, that he did what he did, not for faculty status. He was "the math grunt," the hired hand who filled in with courses that others did not want to teach or that not enough students wanted to learn or that had been the turf of professors who were on sabbatical or had moved on. It didn't take many students to cover the overhead if Brad taught the course. With no benefits, his "position" was cheap to the college.

He did not particularly mind teaching subjects far afield from his own specialty in complex systems modeling. He was the perpetual student. Asked if he could teach a class on anything remotely connected with math or logic, his answer was always yes. And teach he would, even when it meant keeping late hours to stay two chapters ahead of his students. Between Smith, the University of Massachusetts, and Mount Holyoke, he had taught remedial algebra for dunderheads and advanced calculus for would-be engineers; he had taught formal logic to philosophers, operations research to managers, and statistics to social scientists. He had become the go-to guy of Western Massachusetts for any course that looked like it involved symbolic expressions or logical operators of any lineage.

In a perverse way, he had been forced by circumstances into a position tailored to his distractible temperament. He now knew that he never would have been happy pursuing a conventional career in Academia, where, driven by demands to publish and to present, he would have been herded into a narrow box canyon of specialization.

It was the Socratic synergy of teaching and learning that energized him, the tension between knowing and finding out, the delicious interplay of young minds and old ideas.

"If I couldn't teach, I think I would go catatonic. Teaching, learning, always learning: without these, I would just wither like the window-box plants in my apartment. That's why I keep doing this, Emile."

Emile had narrowed his eyes and made a dismissive gesture with his left hand. "Well, then, good for you, I suppose. And good for me. Teaching symbolic logic is not my cup of tea. And it would be such a waste of my talent. A dozen students. Why does the college set the threshold so low on these courses?"

"Because they pay me so little and charge students so much, perhaps?"

"Yes, yes. It always seems to come back to that these days, doesn't it? I don't know what we would do without the likes of you. I don't really know why you do it, Bradley, passionate or principled protestations notwithstanding. Surely, you would be better off in a tenured position."

Surely I would not, he had thought. Some judge would just up the alimony and childcare payments to match my better finances. "I do it for the love of it, Emile. I would still do it even if they didn't pay me. But please, not a word to the administration."

"A vow of silence on the matter." Emile winked as he symbolically zipped his lips in a silly gesture that dated him as surely as his wispy white hair.

◊

An incoming-message tone on Brad's computer brought his attention back to the small kitchen in West Hopeland. It was a message from Angie.

> No Skype video tonight, Daddy. Mom says it is just too much
> like a visit and visits have to be supervised. Sorry. My
> friend Suki said it used to be that way with her dad, but he
> got this big-shot lawyer and got things changed. Maybe
> you should try that.

Yeah, maybe I should find a big-shot lawyer who will take me on as a charity case. He clicked on the green "Video Call" button and waited until the attempt to connect timed out.

Another text message came in:

> Daddy, no video.

"Oh, I didn't realize you meant starting now. I thought I could wait until new papers were served or the Department of Child and Family social workers banged on my apartment door." This he said to the computer screen, but on the keyboard he typed, "My bad" and tapped Enter. The incoming call tone started and he answered—without video.

"How's my Angie?"

"Still your Angie, Daddy. To the max with Spanish homework, going to a dance tomorrow, not talking with Mom. How's by you?"

"What's with you and your mother?"

"This stuff, this no-video crap. I hate her."

"No you don't. You don't hate her. You're just angry with her."

"Hey, I've been in therapy, Dad. I know the rules. You don't get to tell me what I am feeling."

"I am not giving orders or a diagnosis. I'm only labeling the phenomenon. Reframing. Isn't that what Sousa-2-N called it?" Dr. Sousa, once listed with a misspelling as "Sousa, Sousan, PhD" on the building directory where she had her third-floor office, had been relabeled as Sousa-2-N by Brad on their first meeting. She did not have the visually and phonetically playful mind to appreciate his jest, so it had become a private, offline nickname for the therapist who had worked with him and Angie after "the big blow-up." Brad never tired of poking fun at her or at psychotherapists in general. When he was not blaming himself or Grace for his circumstances, he was blaming incompetent psychologists and social workers, with Sousa-2-N at the top of his list.

"Did you say dance? You're going to a dance?"

"Yes, Daddy: D-A-N-C-E, dance."

"With somebody?"

"No, not with 'somebody,' with Kevin."

"'Do I know this Kevin?"

"No, of course not. And you better not use your online skills to try and learn about him."

"Never. That's not the sort of overprotective, helicopter father I am."

"You, a helicopter parent? Was that you in the Huey overhead last night? Circling, interrupting my sleep?"

"Not me, I always use an unmanned drone, near-silent engines. Must have been your Kevin trying to get a peek in your bedroom window."

"Daddy! Please! Mom's home. Watch it."

"What? Has she put nanny software on your iPad now? Or is she listening outside your bedroom door? Forget her; back to Kevin. Frankly, when talking about sixteen-year-old males, worst assumptions are the ones most likely to be accurate."

"Eighteen. He's a senior."

"Then that's it! You are not going."

"Daddy!"

The easy banter continued until a cellphone chimed in the background. "Daddy, I have to go. I have Spanish homework plus a test in AP calc tomorrow."

"And a Kevin waiting on your iPhone. Mustn't make the lad

anxious. My recommendation? Come right out and tell him you don't date older men."

"He's eighteen, Daddy, not thirty."

"Same difference. You can't trust any male past puberty, certainly not an older man." The phone continued to chime in the background.

"Two years, Daddy, two whole years older. And I really have to go."

"Okay, but remember that I warned you about older men. Remember that. It was me who warned you."

It was an unkind and obtuse sarcasm for which there could be no reply. There was no sound on the other end except the continued chiming of the cellphone. Then: "Yeah. I love you, Daddy. Later."

"Love you, too. Have fun at the dance." He stared at the screen as the call ended and a pop-up survey asked him to rate the connection. There was no option for "poignant," so he closed the survey without responding.

four

UNABLE TO GET the unusual student request out of his mind, Brad scrolled again through the list of pending pleas on the InStarTute website. He recognized the handles of some of the students looking for help with homework or asking for a brush-up on one topic or another. As with cab drivers bidding on taxi requests, tutors could respond to anything that suited their moods or backgrounds. They were paid by a complex formula that balanced time spent with each student and the total number of requests served, all weighted by student ratings of the tutor. It did not pay a lot, but it was more than Brad could get flipping burgers at the local BK. And the hiring review for online tutors had been laughably lax. Despite his background, they had let him in.

He preferred to wait until the weekend to work the tutoring site. Weekdays tended to be dominated by last-minute panics over tomorrow's homework or by students looking for someone else to give them the answers. Anyone thinking about mathematics over a weekend was likely to be more serious or in more serious difficulty. Brad had always liked working with students in trouble. He particularly liked working with the younger students in middle and high school, acting as a catalyst, lighting a fire under a future quant wonk, or making the light go on in the heads of girls who had been convinced they couldn't do math. Teaching adolescents would have been his preferred choice if he had a choice. The Web-based service gave him the access he could no longer have in person.

At the very bottom of the Web page, about to be dropped off into tutorial oblivion, was the request from DeTuring. Brad quickly ticked the checkbox next to the post, then clicked the ACCEPT button. An Instant Message box opened, signaling that the student was online at the time.

> TUTOR-10: Hello. So, I take it you're into Turing machines.
>
> DeTuring: there's a prefix. it implies negation or removal
>
> TUTOR-10: OK. So you're not into computational models. How's it going? What do you really want help with?
>
> DeTuring: it's not going, which is why i asked for help. where you been? cant you read? i need help with the four-color theorem.
>
> TUTOR-10: Do you know what the theorem is?
>
> DeTuring: der
>
> TUTOR-10: OK. So, then you should know it's already been proved. Appel and Haken in 1978.
>
> DeTuring: 1976, smart-a, and i know about their crappy, over-complex proof. the other haha proof too using the snark theorem. that is a cheat and parts of that proof are still not published. i already simplified part of the Appel-Haken proof, the reducible configurations. having trouble with the unavoidable-set part.
>
> TUTOR-10: Not surprising; it came to hundreds of pages.
>
> DeTuring: 427. do you really know math? you don't seem too smart. i think i'll drop and rate you a fat zero for this one.
>
> TUTOR-10: OK. But you aren't going to find another tutor better at graph theory.

DeTuring: not using graph theory. i generalized the theorem and reframed the generalization as a computability problem. a little de-turing. LOL. and i use something i developed called canonical reduction theory to map the Thomas's 633 reducible configurations into only 17 special cases. each can be proved by hand because of generalizing. instead of a fat book and a computer program that hardly anyone can understand, i can do it in maybe 40 pages direct. maybe less. no computer program. it's de-turing. follow that?

TUTOR-10: In principle, yes. But I would have to actually take a look at your work so far in order to know whether this is all just a smokescreen of vocab you picked up or you are really onto something. I'm leaning toward the former. What grade are you in?

DeTuring: senior. will drop a PDF in your box. if you can understand it msg me tomorrow. if not f-off

Brad tried to focus on the topology take-homes, but his mind kept drifting to the four-color theorem. Could a high school kid have done something that had eluded some of the best mathematical minds of the world: a direct, simple proof that no more than four colors are required to unambiguously color any possible flat map? The original proof had required a complex computer program, thousands of hours of computation, and a serpentine logical argument hundreds of pages long. There were still mathematicians who questioned that proof and thought that there might be undiscovered errors lurking in it. Others had since improved on the computer algorithms, but the basic line of attack remained.

If what the kid claimed was true, he was a genius. If not, what was the scam about? Brad stayed logged in at InStarTute and kept checking his dropbox. He was slowly becoming convinced that the kid was bullshitting. At half-past eleven, Brad was about to pack it in for the night when one last check showed a waiting item in his dropbox. The attached note read:

> sorry. had to fix spelling and punct. also found missing close paren in expression 13.9 and a spurious subset sign in 23.2

The PDF file took some time to download. Brad opened it and paged down through it: forty-nine single-spaced pages of numbered paragraphs interspersed with displayed formulae.

He started back at the beginning, reading the stiff, formal language aloud: "Given any finite or infinite planar map on any closed or open surface, consider a coloring such that . . ."

It was nearly three in the morning when he shut his laptop and straightened the pile of penciled notes he had created. He still didn't know whether the kid was deluded or on his way to fame, but the proof was definitely not a joke. It was too early to tell whether it was correct or not—reading mathematics was not like reading a short story—but the general outline of the argument seemed sound. It would take a meticulous, line-by-line and term-by-term review, perhaps by better minds than Brad's, to know whether it had genuine merit. Particularly problematic was the idiosyncratic notation that DeTuring had introduced for his new theoretical framework, which was at the core of the ability to compress so many exceptions into a handful of special cases.

Too tired even to trudge down the hall to the bedroom, Brad curled up on the couch and pulled the afghan over himself. In minutes he was asleep, dreaming of floating formulae and exotic expressions vomiting from the mouth of a sweet-faced young boy who kept following after him and tapping on his shoulder. The taps hurt.

five

ARMAND WAS BACK, smiling and ruddy-cheeked as he entered Mandy's and stomped his boots on the sisal mat just inside the door. Patrons looked up from their checkers, puzzles, and newspapers as he strode across the uneven wide-board flooring toward the alcove. There, an addition joined what had once been a worker's cottage to form the intellectual and social nexus of the small town. Armand shoved one of the round, walnut-and-maple inlaid tables against the two already occupied and pulled up a green bentwood chair. His grin broadened.

Everyone was eager to learn about his visit and his new boyfriend, and he knew it. But nobody would break protocol to ask. Instead, Brad kicked things off by mentioning his newfound math wizard and musing about the nature of Intelligence. One of the relative newcomers, a psychologist whose name Brad kept forgetting, raised the issue of general intelligence, the so-called G-factor. Brad interrupted. "It's not a scalar. It's a vector in N-space," he said. "A composition of multiple dimensions, many factors."

Armand leaned forward. "Why limit yourself to a vector, how about a region in N-space?"

"Okay, guys." Gillian spread two newly-tanned arms on the table.

"For the legally blonde in your midst, are you saying that Intelligence comes in different forms?"

"No." Brad sketched an invisible shape on the table with his finger. "I don't know what they are saying. Maybe they don't know either. What I am now saying is that there are different factors in Intelligence, that any one person has different amounts of these components or capabilities. I'm good at logical thinking, poor at reading maps. I can manipulate four-dimensional shapes in my head but have trouble getting up my three-dimensional stairs. Different abilities."

"Is stair-climbing ability a form of intelligence?"

"Spatial awareness and manipulation, maybe. But the point was about different cognitive capabilities: verbal intelligence, logical reasoning, and so forth."

Tom Carraway, the old man of the group, leaned forward, bobbing his bald head as he talked. "Well, look, it's clear that some people are only really smart in some ways or about some things, while others seem to have a broad brilliance in many different domains or . . . or modes of mental manipulation."

"M&M&Ms."

"Mental manipulation modes."

"Manifest mental manipulation modes."

"Multiple manifest mental manipulation modes."

"Okay, okay. All I am saying—"

"Like emotional intelligence and—"

"Emotional intelligence in quotes. It's hardly an established construct. And the science is weak." The repartee bounced at random around the clustered tables, thrown like stew vegetables and seasoning into a common campfire pot.

"What I am getting at is that there are people who are brilliant, but not broadly so, only in certain narrowly defined areas or ways. And there are others who are—"

"Polymaths."

"Or dilettantes."

"Not the same thing at all. A true polymath—"

"A renaissance man." Brad looked at Gillian. "Or woman."

"Thank you."

"—is not a dabbler in diverse diversions but accomplished at, demonstrating—"

"Mastery. Mastery of multiple manifest mental manipulation modes in many multifaceted—"

"Enough, already." Brad made a time-out sign. "I really was interested in something more specific. I have this kid, a boy genius, possibly."

Tom drew back and scowled. "I thought you had a daughter?"

"I am not talking personally. There's this high school kid online who may have solved a problem that has challenged some of the best mathematical minds for over a hundred-and-fifty years. He—"

"An idiot savant?"

"Well, the savant part, yes. I don't know if his proof of the Four-Color Theorem is correct, but—"

"It's been done. Long ago." The dismissive drop-and-run response from Clarence Endicott, a civil engineer with a dark and deeply lined face, was typical of his contributions.

"I know, and this kid knows, but that original proof was brute force, some would say clumsy and complicated. If I am right, this high school senior has created a solution that is truly elegant."

"Define elegant."

With that, the Coconut Club jumped the track to a side spur focused on Elegance before chugging on to the equally elusive Simplicity. They did not get back to the subject of mathematical genius until it was nearly time to adjourn to the Mohegan Diner, where the layout with small booths and a long, stool-studded counter would limit the conversation.

Armand turned to Brad as they were all collecting their coats. "I'm afraid we've been 'detouring' some from your interest." He winked.

Brad was surprised. "You know this kid? You know, his online handle is 'DeTuring.'"

"Yes, I know. I've seen his posts on InStarTute."

"I didn't know you—"

"Yeah, I helped found the site, in fact. I'm on the Board and do oversight. Made some pocket change when we sold it off to Peterson Online. If I had held out, I might have scored even bigger. I'm good with mathematics but sometimes not so much with arithmetic, particularly when the numbers are preceded by those devilish double-barred Ss. Still, I have managed to add to my inheritance, where as you never had anything and seem to be on a downward fiscal trend from there. We can only hope you die poor but happy, although in your case I am only confident about the first part."

◊

At the Mohegan, a classic aluminum-sheathed railway-car diner and local landmark, Brad ended up opposite Gillian in a red-leatherette booth for two tucked at the far end. Conversation dwindled to isolated words and nods as they both dug into the pot roast special with whipped potatoes and garden peas. Over coffee, Brad found himself studying her face, watching the way her sparse blonde eyebrows twitched with thought and how the fingers of her smile lines flickered in and out of existence. She looked up at him and said, "What?"

"You're a lawyer, right?" he stammered, quickly shifting from his deep inspection of her face.

"Last time I looked in the mirror, yes."

"So what kind of law do you do?"

"Real estate."

"Somehow I got the impression you did the Perry Mason sort of thing, a trial lawyer."

"Did. Once. I started out in the Middlesex County DA's office, prosecuting drug dealers and other miscellaneous miscreants. When I left, I was ready for something that made sense, where simple logic prevailed, if not always, at least mostly. I was tired of seeing the il-logic of over-grown street kids with priors doing hard time because they had inept defense and pimps who trafficked in minors walking because of some slip-up in the chain of evidence or adept maneu-vering by some defense shyster. So I walked."

"Why real estate?"

"Real estate law is simpler, far less demanding. The lines are clear but, for the most part, it's not about good guys and bad guys. And it pays a hell of a lot better. Despite what you see around you"—her gesture swept the room—"there's a lot of money in this part of the state and a lot of titles that are as fuzzy as wooly-bear caterpillars."

"You're not married?"

"You hitting on me, Brad?"

"No, I . . ."

"Dang."

"I mean, I . . ."

"I was married. To a cop. Killed in the line of duty. Sideswiped as he stepped out of his patrol car to check on a speeder just pulled over."

"I'm sorry."

"I'm not. Don't get me wrong. I was not glad that he was killed, but I was glad that it was over. It wasn't working. He had a temper, and I had already filed for divorce. As fickle fortune would have it, I was still the beneficiary on his insurance. So I used the money to move out here, bought out a practice, and now get to argue easements and zoning exemptions and then trot off for winter vacations in St. Thomas. Does that sound uncaring? It was a long time ago, a very long time."

"I understand. You can't hold onto the feelings forever."

"You're divorced, too, right?"

"Right. Also a long time ago." They both nodded in unison, a slow, rhythmic rocking that said they were through with that topic and ready to return to discussing Genius and the myth of the *wunderkind* or whether Mozart really could compose a symphony in his head in a single minute. When they finished, they were the last of the Club to leave the diner, everyone else having discreetly given them the space to talk about nothing.

"I'll pick up the check," she said. "You go ahead."

"No, I can't let you do that. I should pay. It's about time."

"You can let me do that. It's not like we're on a date, where old-fashioned chivalry is still permitted to lurk on occasion. I got it. You go ahead. I'll see you next Thursday."

six

EMMA WAITED IN THE ARMCHAIR. Bright sun from the window behind her haloed her wispy hair. She looked up from the magazine that she had been staring at without reading, almost without seeing. "Hello? Who are you?" It was a simple query, more curiosity than challenge.

The room smelled faintly of lemons or oranges, the generic citrus of institutional disinfectant. For a moment, the perfume rising from the roses in Brad's hand struggled with the scent before melting into an olfactory mélange.

"It's me, Mom." He laid the roses on the bedside table. "I came to see you. First Monday of the month."

"Oh, Brad, I am so glad you came back. You know, I was so worried you wouldn't make it back before the baby was born."

"Mom, it's me, Bradley, your son, Bradley. Not your Brad. He didn't make it, Mom. You know that."

"What do you mean, didn't make it. Here you are, big as life. You're home. And handsome as ever. How I have missed you." Her mouth closed into a line as she blinked back tears.

"Mom, I know it's hard for you to remember and keep things straight, but he was killed before I was born."

Her face became an animated mix of confusion and frustration. "I saw the pictures on the television. The embassy in Saigon, the helicopters. Everyone got out. I've been waiting."

Brad knelt in front of her and took her hand, giving it an extra squeeze as he looked up into her eyes—eyes so bright, alert—a disguise. "Mom, I never knew him. You always said I look like him, but for me there were only the pictures." The Fall of Saigon had been one of the legends of Brad's youth, a story made personal and relevant because he had been born just as the last of the American embassy personnel were being evacuated, just as his father, a Marine guard, had become one of the last American casualties of the war. "I'm your son."

She studied his face, licking her lips in concentration. "Of course, you are. I am so glad you decided to visit."

"I always do, Mom. Every month."

She leaned to peer around him. "Where's Grace and the baby? Are they parking the car?"

"The baby is fifteen years old, and Grace is remarried, Mom. You keep forgetting.'

"How silly of me. Yes, I keep forgetting. I don't know what goes on in this old gray head of mine. I'm just a muddle-headed wombat, it seems."

Brad rose and kissed her forehead. "I'll never forget you reading the stories to me. *The Muddle-Headed Wombat. Pumpkin Paddy and the Bunyip.* Great stories. Someday. Someday I'll go there, see where you and all those stories came from."

"It will be a distant someday on what you make, my part-time professor." She tousled his hair. "How many courses are you teaching this semester?" It was like the lights coming up in a theater at intermission. Suddenly she was back in the brightly lit present.

"Just the one, Mom, an advanced seminar at Smith. And some guest shots at the University."

"Topology? Or is this that formal logic stuff again? Belief revision and the falsifiability of theory. That stuff?"

"No, not 'that stuff,' thank God. No, this is straight topology and geometry. Except not straight, since we're exploring non-Euclidian spaces."

"Nice one. A mathematical in-joke. I can still remember teaching you about parallel lines that meet. Your mouth was as round as a pie and your eyes as big."

"You were a good teacher, Mom. You were the one who lit the spark in me. A good teacher.

"Was I? I don't remember, really. What did I teach?"

"High school algebra and AP calculus, Mom."

"Really?"

"Really. And you taught me to love thinking things through, focusing, not being distracted. Except you have a distractible son. 'Pay attention, Brad! Stay focused.' And your favorite: 'Be. Here. Now.' You were the only mathematician I ever knew to quote Baba Ram Dass."

"Richard Alpert."

"Right. Sharp as ever, Mom."

"Here. Now. At least for now."

They laughed quietly together, then fell into easy conversation that bounced from the ever-interesting, ever-changing residents at the Brookwood Home to the brain-dead deadlock in the House of Representatives and on to the challenges of teaching Riemannian geometry. Then, suddenly, the intermission was over, the house lights dimmed once more, and Emma was lost in the dark again.

"Where are you living, Brad?"

"West Hopeland."

"And where is that? Is it in Queensland?"

"No, not Australia. Here in Massachusetts."

"This is Massachusetts? Feels like Tasmania. Or . . . I don't know.

When do you have to go back to the base? Shouldn't they discharge you, now that the war is over, now that we lost?"

Brad tried to bring her back to the present, but she only got more confused and agitated, her voice rising into a shrill warble that brought a nurse from the hall.

"Are you all right, Mrs. Williams?"

"Yes, of course. I'm right, but this man is mad as a gumtree full of galahs." In her frustration, she reached back to the idioms of her Australian youth. "I'll thank you to see the bloke out."

The nurse gave Brad a knowing look and shook her head.

"Maybe it's time for me to go, Mom. I need to get over to the college, then return Armand's car to him. I'll see you next month."

"I should hope not. When my husband gets back from Vietnam, he'll teach you some manners. He's a Marine, you know."

Brad's head drooped. "I love you, Mom."

"What?"

"I said, I love you."

"Oh. I love you, too. Be careful, darling. Please write. And please come back."

"I will. I will."

In the hallway, Brad spotted the nurse about to push through the double doors into the next wing. "Cynthia, wait up a second. What can you tell me about my mother?"

"Mrs. Williams? She's doing fine: healthy, blood pressure under control, eating well."

"Not what I meant."

"Mentally, she's in and out. Today seemed to be one of her good days, yesterday, not so good. It's the way with Alzheimer's—up and down—but the downs dip lower and lower. I wish we could be more optimistic. At least she can still manage self-care, so for now she can stay in the assisted-living wing."

"For now."

"What can I say? Your mother is still better off than a lot of the residents."

"Still." There was no response. "Thanks. I know you are doing your best, doing well by her. It is just so hard to see such a bright mind so dimmed, so . . . so muddled."

◊

Brad's driving tended to follow his mood, which was down enough so that traffic backed up behind him in the no-passing zones of the narrow roads. He ended up late for his seminar at Smith.

All through the discussion of Riemannian geometry, he kept flashing on images of his mother as a young woman, teaching her school-age son non-Euclidian geometry between lectures on organic farming and stories of life on the Gold Coast of Australia peppered with the endless retelling of meeting this handsome American backpacking his way through New South Wales and Queensland.

In the back of the seminar room, the raccoon-eyed Sophia spent the time texting.

seven

By the following week, the IMs with DeTuring had grown into a nightly ritual. Reviewing and correcting the proof was slow-going, tedious work full of detours and backtracking, a switchback uphill trudge made all the harder by the limitations of the medium that linked them. The InStarTute website had a shared sketchpad tool that allowed the student and tutor to make and share simple line drawings, construct displayed formulae using basic mathematical symbols and conventions, and even to do limited freehand sketching, but it was clumsy to use with a mouse or touchpad and not well-adapted to the more advanced level of dialogue in which Brad and DeTuring were engaged. After two weeks, they had worked their way through only the first eleven pages, and DeTuring was getting both impatient and defensive.

DeTuring: it's obvious.

TUTOR-10: It is not obvious. You can't merely assert it; you have to prove it. Every step along the way. And in this case you can't.

DeTuring: i can too

TUTOR-10: No, because you can't apply the grump operator

to that Local Embedded Region. BTW, why did you call that squiggle a grump operator?

DeTuring: group and lump, obviously

TUTOR-10: Obviously. Anyway that operation on the LER is impossible.

DeTuring: it seems fine to me

TUTOR-10: Draw it.

DeTuring: why? i can picture it in my head

TUTOR-10: Convert it to a digraph, then draw it, no crossing lines.

There was a long delay.

DeTuring: oh, i can't

TUTOR-10: Right, because it's non-planar. I know you think the proof is shortened by working in your notation, but you need to keep checking your work by going back to graphs and graph theory.

DeTuring: so the proof is wrong

TUTOR-10: No, that step is wrong. Find another way to get from 6.1 to 6.3. Sleep on it. Something will come to you.

DeTuring: i don't sleep much.

TUTOR-10: At your age, you need the sleep.

DeTuring: i sleep in study hall. that's enough. you're not my mother.

TUTOR-10: No, just your friend.

DeTuring: really?

TUTOR-10: Well, of a sort. A tutor-friend.

DeTuring: you ever wonder about the kids you tutor?

TUTOR-10: Wonder what?

DeTuring: you know, their lives, stuff

TUTOR-10: Sometimes. In your case, I already know some. Like you don't do anything but math and you don't sleep.

DeTuring: i sleep. and i do stuff

TUTOR-10: What stuff? Any sports? Exercise helps the brain, you know.

DeTuring: lacrosse. not anymore. outgrew the outfit and no money for new one. you?

TUTOR-10: Downhill. But lift tickets are so expensive and the snow sucks, so not this year. Look, kid, get some sleep.

Brad closed the browser and took a sip of the tea that had grown cold. He knew he was almost crossing a line. This was not mathematics, not online tutoring. However casual the exchange, the site had strict rules about personal information and communication. All exchanges were permanently logged, a record of exactly what was said, presumably archived against future need in the event of accusations or legal action.

But what kind of a seventeen-year-old lived and breathed math, spent hours nearly every evening texting with a disembodied tutor, and slept at school? Leave it alone, Brad, he told himself. Don't take chances.

But he didn't leave it, and the next several sessions all ended with more quick asides and small personal disclosures in the closing snippets.

. . .

DeTuring: gotta go, jack's home

TUTOR-10: Brother?

DeTuring: stepbrother, works after school

TUTOR-10: Is he smart like you?

DeTuring: smart enough but not like me

TUTOR-10: Oh. CU.

. . .

TUTOR-10: Did you finish the revision to page 13?

DeTuring: no, 2 much homework 2 do. stupid calc. boring. 2

easy. hate it

. . .

DeTuring: cannot understand LA

TUTOR-10: LA?

DeTuring: language arts

TUTOR-10: Can you get your mom or dad to help?

DeTuring: mom left years ago. dad's a dunce, does plumbing, construction work. when he works

. . .

DeTuring: we need to cut it short tonite

TUTOR-10: Okay.

DeTuring: hanging out w/ math homies

TUTOR-10: Good. I'll be online tomorrow if you want to continue figuring out how to prove that lemma. CU.

The flag on the dialogue said the student had switched to a chat room. Impulsively, Brad opened the ROLE dropdown at the top of the page to select MONITOR and clicked the CHATROOM tab on the side. DeTuring, MODler, GeekGirl13, and Avatar18 were listed as logged in.

MODler: hey reg, whassup?

DeTuring: nothing, still headbanging that proof

GeekGirl13: You never give up, do you Reg?

DeTuring: nope

MODler: u do the math olys again this year reg?

DeTuring: nope. busy. gotta finish the proof. don't need 2 prove anything with the national olys. last year was enuff. been there done that. u try that notation yet?

MODler: ya, not sure about the grump operator

DeTuring: reread the paper. it's simple

MODler: 2 u maybe brainiac

DeTuring: just smarter than u

Brad tabbed back to the requests list with his heart racing. The kid's name was Reg. He had been in the Mathematics Olympiad. And the word cyber-stalking flashed briefly in Brad's mind. However reluctant he might be to admit it, he had grown immensely curious about this bright student whose handle was DeTuring, who talked about higher math abstractions and logic as easily as the denizens of the Coconut Club shredded semantics and philosophy.

Who was this kid? What was his story? What did he look like? Brad started from what he knew. The kid was a senior in some Massachusetts high school, taking AP calculus and finding it too easy to bother about. He had last year been on the team that represented Massachusetts at the Math Olympiad. Brad searched out articles online about "Math Olympiad" and "Massachusetts." Halfway down the first results page was a link to an article in an Eastern Mass local paper. The short piece was topped by a posed photo on the broad steps of some school.

Amidst the forced smiles and stiff poses, one face drew his attention. It might as well have been the only colorized figure in an otherwise black-and-white photo. At the right end of the second row, a girl, with a dimpled smile like a lighthouse beacon, looked into the camera with dark, intelligent eyes that were both challenging and inviting. "I am!" they asserted. "Reckon with me." She stood, feet planted apart, slightly distanced from the girl next to her. By height, she should have been with the shorter kids in the front row, but she had clearly chosen her spot rather than acceding to convention or the directions of the unseen photographer.

Brad's eyes dropped to the caption and scanned the names of students in the second row. At the end was Gina Bellingham, Ipswich, MA. Gina, he thought. Maybe short for Regina. Reg. Was the amazing DeTuring a girl? She reminded Brad of his own daughter, more handsome than pretty, but this girl's short, boyish hair added to an almost androgynous impression. Her swarthy complexion suggested Hispanic or Middle Eastern bloodlines.

Brad printed the page as a PDF, then thought better of it and deleted the file, then printed it again. He zoomed in on the girl's face. Except for the darker skin, she might have passed for Angie's sister, that and her deep, brown-black eyes. Those eyes, so fierce, slightly narrowed, feline, seductive. Brad closed the file almost reluctantly.

eight

BRAD'S TEACHING KEPT HIM away from the tutoring site for several days. When next he logged in, instead of seeing the reassuring blue and white of the Teacher homepage, he was greeted by a red-bordered message box headed "Important Notice!!" with two exclamation points and a line to underscore the importance. He was about to dismiss it without reading, convinced that anything that depended on such excessive punctuation to make its point was not worthy of his attention, but his eye was caught by a word in the middle of the box that stood out as if it were rendered in boldface: "inapropriate." Brad was constitutionally incapable of missing a misspelled word. He quickly read the message and spotted another typo at the end of the last sentence.

> Registered Tutors are reminded that they are bound both by the signed Contract for Services and the published Terms of Service (see link below). Tutors are recommended to periodically review both the ToS and their CfS. In particular, unacceptable language and inapropriate communication between Tutors and Student members will not be tolerated and is grounds for termination of the CfS

and followup.

It was signed with more spurious punctuation: "Malcolm Todd and Your InStarTutes' Team." The notice was so badly written that Brad started to compose an email railing against rampant illiteracy and the amateurish example this set for a site that was trying to reach impressionable students. He stopped at the word "amateurish" and wondered whether the message had, in fact, originated with the site management. Was it broadcast or was he being targeted?

Paranoia, Brad. Are you ready to add that to your list of personal diagnoses, just before "personality disorder" and right after "manic-depressive"? As he stared at the message, it began to look more and more like the work of some student. Perhaps the site had been hacked. Uncertain and anxious, he posted his own notice that he was offline indefinitely then logged out.

◊

With a midterm exam to write and a series of guest lectures in one of Armand's School of Nursing classes to prepare, Brad stayed off-line most of the week. When he finally checked in, DeTuring was not logged in, but there was a message from her waiting in his Inbox.

> this sucks. you are not around and i can't call you. where are you? my hand hurts and i am trying to type this to some jerk-off teach who doesn't care. i'm going to downrate you so bad you will never get paid.

Brad tapped REPLY and typed his message.

> I care. I've been busy. But I have thought about the problem we had with that lemma. I'll stay logged in tonight. Ping me when you are online.

◊

The notes for his first guest spot filled only half a page when an insistent beeping told him to switch to his browser window. DeTuring was online. Regina.

DeTuring: about time, teach
TUTOR-10: Like I said, it's been a busy week.
DeTuring: you got family?
TUTOR-10: Not here.
DeTuring: divorced?
TUTOR-10: Yeah. Want to do some math?
DeTuring: no. let's talk
TUTOR-10: This is a math tutoring site.
DeTuring: can we IM? Skype?
TUTOR-10: It's against the rules.
DeTuring: f the rules. this is 2 f-ing hard
TUTOR-10: That's how it works. Want to work on the proof?
DeTuring: no. f-off jerkoff

◊

"So, your brilliant boy is a genius girl." Armand had arrived early at Mandy's, giving Brad a few minutes with him alone. "And there's more to the story. Let me guess. You have the hots for this teenage reincarnation of Ada Lovelace."

"No. I do not have the hots for her. You know better than that. You know the whole story with me."

"Hey, no need to get defensive. We all can get a hard-on now and then for some cute adolescent. Doesn't mean anything, doesn't have to go anywhere. Got a picture?"

"I thought you were into boys."

"Men. Mostly. But I was a horny adolescent once, too, just like the rest of the gang. Some of them still are, even with receding hairlines. No offence. And, yes, I tried a lot of things, even had experiences on both sides of the bed. A cute ass is a cute ass on either sex."

"I had no idea, Armand."

Armand gave him an acutely skewed smile. "So it's not lust, you claim. Then what is it?"

"I'm concerned. Something is going on. Suddenly, she is not interested in mathematical proofs. She wants to talk. I think there's some kind of trouble."

"She wants to talk? That's what females want. A teenage girl losing interest in math? I thought that was the developmental norm."

"Not normal in this girl's case. As I told you before, she's brilliant. She is passionate about this proof. Then, suddenly, she wants to talk—and not about math."

"You know you can put an alert on her record. It goes to her school and the guidance office follows up."

"I know, but I don't want to do that. You know how kids this age work. She would see it as betrayal. She'd know it was me who sent the alert. Besides, I have nothing to go on. And besides that, the last thing I want to do is draw attention to myself in that kind of situation. You understand."

"Oh, I do. As a bisexual who taught for years at an all-boys Catholic prep school, I can tell you that even facing too long in the wrong direction can get you into trouble. No, you, of all people, do not want to attract the scrutiny of the Mass Department of Child and Family Services. State-employed social workers are, as a species, underpaid, under-qualified, and over-reactive. I would just leave it alone and hope it's nothing."

"I don't think I can. This girl is something special."

"I'm sure. But here comes Tom and Gillian, with the rest of the Club no doubt close behind. I would drop this and switch topics, if I were you. Gillian, our resident lawyer and feminist of a certain age, just might turn her forensic forces on you."

Tom, catching only the word feminist from across the room, launched the first Topic of Today even as he sat down: The Fall of Feminism. Gillian kicked at his chair playfully but with enough impact to shake the foam on the caffè latte he held. He licked the foam from where it had spattered onto his wrist and launched into a highly original history of gender politics in post-modern America. It was he who bore the brunt of Gillian's courtroom-honed debate techniques for the rest of the afternoon. Brad stayed out of the line of fire.

On the way out of Mandy's, Gillian caught up with him. "What's up with your boy math genius?"

"Girl. Turns out he's a she. And she seems to have moved on to other things. Maybe has a boyfriend. Who knows."

"What a pity. It sounded like she was headed somewhere at a young age."

"Yeah. That's what I thought, too. You headed for the Mohegan?"

"Not tonight. I've reached my annual quota on pork chops and gravy, roast beef and gravy, meatloaf and gravy, or gravy and gravy. And I will be just fine if I never see another scoop of watery whipped potatoes. I was thinking of pizza. Wanna join me?"

"Er, sure. Why not. But it's my treat."

"Oh, no you don't. I asked you. Feminist rules: I ask, I buy."

"Okay, you win. Never argue with a feminist lawyer armed with a rule book."

"Or with an older woman."

"You, Gillian, do not qualify as an older woman."

"Older than you, young man, older than you. You want to walk or drive? I was thinking of the new Flatbread's. It's at the other end of town."

"That's what, all of a mile or so?"

"One point two, traffic light to traffic light. In real estate you know these details of local geography. Are you up for it?"

"I'll race you."

"Not fair, I'm still in work clothes, and this skirt is too straight."

"Pity."

◊

Over glasses of a New Hampshire Baco Noir wine and "wood-fired pizza of roasted peppers and eggplant topped with local goat cheese and an olivini tapenade," they talked about kids and young people. "No, I don't have kids," she said. "At first, we knew we were too young. Then, we knew we were too old. Doors close and you stop listening for visitors."

"You're hardly too old, Gillian. There's still time."

"Easy for a man to say. A woman has a different sense of time, and my alarm clock is already ringing, saying wake up, woman, and welcome to middle age. Menopause arrives any afternoon now."

"You're kidding. You're not that old. You're what? Not quite forty?"

"You're being so very generous. It's the dim light in here. And the wine. Try eight, Brad, forty-eight. I am less than two years shy of the big five-oh and no man in my life and no kids. I . . . I am sorry. It's the wine."

"No apologies, please. Your turn will come someday."

"Someday. Someday my prince will come? Right. He'll take one look, call me 'Ma'am,' and hit on his super-Christian neighbor across the street."

"Are you talking about Jenna? Jesus H. Jehovah-loving Jenna and her dimwitted dog?"

"No, I was speaking generically. But your neighbor is certainly one evangelical phenom."

"You've met her?"

"Who in town hasn't? She is not one to waste an opportunity to try and save a heathen soul."

"Is that what you are? Heathen?"

"I suppose, if secular Jews qualify. My family were pork-eating apostates, lawyers all, but still proud of our Hebrew heritage. What about you? Are you on your way to succumbing to Saint Jenna?"

"I had enough of that growing up. My grandmother was a religious fanatic whose efforts to fan the flames of religious fervor soured me on the whole lot. I believe in mathematics and the brotherhood of mathematicians and worship only at the altar of logic. And logic tells me it is time to wind it up here. The wait-staff has been eyeing us impatiently."

"Look, I'll drive you home."

"Your car is in back of the Muffin and Mug, Gillian. I live two blocks beyond."

"Then I'll walk you home. The air will do me good."

"Okay, but I pick up the tab."

"Okay."

Brad looked surprised for a second, then picked up the folded check tented on the table. "When did pizza get so expensive?" he mumbled.

"You manage it?"

"Yeah." He put a twenty and a ten on the table, then swapped the ten for another twenty. Being a gentleman had become costly, he concluded.

When he caught up with Gillian, she was standing under the light in the parking lot, looking elegant in her straight skirt, high boots, and tailored jacket. He wanted to compliment her, but didn't know whether her feminist credentials would allow it.

They walked in silence in the middle of the street to avoid the still-icy sidewalks. At the steps to Brad's apartment, she gave him a long hug. "Thanks. It was fun."

Brad responded with an extra squeeze. "Yeah, it was. See you next week at Mandy's."

◊

Noting Gillian and Brad's hike toward Flatbread's, Armand had extricated himself from the group heading for the Mohegan Diner. He picked up his Ferrari in the marked-off bit of the bank parking lot where he always left it, safe from the risk of some clueless driver putting a ding in it. He drove one-handed, spinning the steering wheel with the palm of his hand as he sped out of town, snaking the secondary roads like a rally driver until he reached the row of junipers signaling the steep, switchback driveway up to the dark, sprawling house that he called home. The floodlights came on as he approached, and the far left garage door swung up after he tapped the remote on the dashboard. With Steve away on a flight, he had the house to himself.

He headed first for the home theater where he poured himself a snifter of Armagnac from the bar before slipping his Macbook Air from its leather case and waking it up. He used his extra set of credentials to access the administrative tools of the InStarTute site. There she was, Brad's math maiden, DeTuring, a student at Ipswich High School, full name: Regina Elizabeth Josephson Bellingham. And there was her student photo. He enlarged it.

"Very sweet, Regina. Absent the dimples and the bangle earrings you would remind me of Romero. Sweet boy, Romero. We had fun in Venezuela, we did. He was very bright, too, but he didn't have the advantages of being born in the U S of A, and there was only so much I could do. And then . . . Well, there are things in life that are best unrecalled. Secrets. From yourself. Many secrets, Regina. What are yours? Or are you too young to have secrets yet? Could I help you collect some, some you will want to recall? Or will it be my nerdy friend Bradley Williams who gives you stories to store away?"

He set a flag on the record in the database so he could go directly back to it as needed, logged out, and closed the laptop. He cupped his hand around the bowl of the snifter and swirled the Armagnac, letting the sweet-almond essence take him back again, to his life before Steve.

Steve was very committed and very possessive. He did not want to know too much about Armand's past, but he had a lot to say on the subject of Armand's future. "We shall see, Steve."

nine

BRAD HAD LEFT HIS LAPTOP open on the kitchen table. When he tapped a key, it woke up, open to the InStarTute homepage. He logged in again and on the tutor homepage the "student waiting" flag was flashing on the bannerhead.

DeTuring: my hand's better. let's pound some proof

TUTOR-10: What happened to your hand?

DeTuring: punched a wall with it, broke my thumb

TUTOR-10: You need to keep your thumb on the outside.

DeTuring: now someone tells me

TUTOR-10: Why a wall?

DeTuring: it was behind jack. i missed the a-hole and landed one on the bedroom wall

TUTOR-10: Your brother, right?

DeTuring: stepbrother

TUTOR-10: Right. Ready to get to work?

DeTuring: ok, but it is so f-ing slow like this. we should both be standing in front of a whiteboard

TUTOR-10: Yeah, that would be better, but this is what we have.

The argument over a method of attack for the next stage of the proof had gone back and forth for nearly an hour when the girl suddenly changed the subject.

DeTuring: i know who you are now. you live in South Hadley

Brad's heart thumped wildly and his vision narrowed into a cone. His hands hesitated over the keyboard.

TUTOR-10: Wrong. Must be some other tutor.
DeTuring: no, i know. you teach at Smith

Brad started to type "How do you know?" but backspaced over it.

TUTOR-10: What makes you think that?
DeTuring: topology, graph theory, you mentioned formal logic. you're on the part-time instructor list. and you are the only one who answered my help request. i tracked you down with google. not hard. i'm a genius remember

What next, he thought. Break it off, now, completely. Quit InStarTute, be ready to move out-of-state. No, save the panic for later, just end it now.

TUTOR-10: I can't help you anymore. Good luck. Bye.

He logged out of the site, closed his browser, and powered down the laptop, as if stopping the flow of electrons would stop his rising panic. He shook his hands at his side and took deep breaths as he stood and turned in a slow, ritual circle. As usual, a stack of accumulated dishes waited in the sink. Time to pretend you are not living the life of a scruffy bachelor, he told himself. Keep yourself busy and forget about this. He rolled up his sleeves.

Getting the dried-on crust off his plates and removing the plastic milk-and-coffee scum coating the bottom of his coffee mugs kept him occupied. As he finally finished drying the last of the dishes, his cellphone buzzed in his pocket. He wiped his hands on his jeans and answered. "Yo."

"Is this Bradley Williams?" It was a husky, Demi Moore voice. "This is DeTuring."

The kitchen started to shimmer before his eyes. "How? How did you get this number?"

"If I can prove the four-color theorem, you think tracking down some stupid tutor is going to slow me down?"

"You cannot call me. You have to understand that. I am serious."

"And you think I'm not? We have to meet."

"We can't. We can't meet. However much I may want to—you may want to—we can't."

"We have to. I need to finish this proof, and the website sucks big-time. A few long weekends and we can finish this sucker."

"What's the hurry? So what if it takes a while. You have years."

"I don't have years. I graduate in May. This is an exercise, a warm-up, a training session. I need to finish it and move on, on to the Millennium Prize."

Brad shook with laughter. "And you said you were serious."

"I am. One million dollars serious. The Millennium Prize. I was going to tackle the Poincaré Conjecture. I was close to seeing a way through, but that Russian psycho case got there first and then turned down the money. What an idiot!"

"Grigoriy Perelman is an oddball, true, a reclusive and eccentric genius if ever there was one. But just because he turned down both the Fields Medal and the Millennium Prize does not qualify him as psychotic."

"Who cares? He got there first. Now, I can't waste time. I'm worried somebody else will solve P versus NP."

"Interesting choice, that." Brad laughed again. "Why?"

"Because I think I can do it. Because it matters. It's one of the few Millennium problems with immediate, real-world consequences.

What do you think? What's your guess? Are P and NP equivalent?"

"Well, if they're not, it's a real blow to computer science. Messes up game theory, cryptography, artificial intelligence. Some interesting problems might take universe lifetimes to compute the answers."

"You're not talking to one of your rich retards in college. I know what P versus NP is about. I just wanted to know what you thought. That HP guy thought he nailed it a couple years ago."

"You mean Vinay Deolalikar and his discredited proof?"

"Yeah, whatever. I could see when his paper came out where he went wrong. Now I just want to get on with it."

"So, if you're worried somebody might get there first, why don't you just start working directly on the problem? It's a very active area, with lots of players already in the game."

"I need practice. That's why I am using computation theory on the four-color problem. And I need help. We need to meet."

"No."

"This is the most important thing in the world to me. This is my ticket. I already paid for it. I want to use it, to get out of jail free. You don't know what it's like."

"No, I don't. But you can get help. Whatever it is, there are people who can help."

"Who? Social workers? Therapists? A bunch of manipulative, deceptive . . . No."

"Okay, no. But I really can't work with you anymore. I have classes to teach, I . . ."

"I can come out there. I know it's Hopeland, not South Hadley. West Hopeland. The IP address for your computer was misleading. My friend Phoebe—you know her as GeekGirl13—is a computer hacker. She has been helping me track you down. I can come to your place, and we can work on the proof, and then I can leave you alone."

"No. I said no. I would like to help you, believe me. I would absolutely love to meet you and to work with you. Maybe someday, but it is just not in the cards now. So, please don't call me again." He hung up and held the button until the phone powered down. He set it on the table, then lifted his shaking hands to his face.

He could hear his heart pounding, almost drowning out the voice in his head. You want to do this, don't you, Bradley. You want to meet her. "No, I can't." Find a way. She needs you. Make it happen. "No. Not this time."

He left the relative warmth of the kitchen and headed to the chilly bedroom. Under the duvet and worn wool coverlet, Brad shivered and fell into a troubled sleep, with dreams of Regina, outside his door, knocking. When he opened the door, she was standing there naked, shivering, trying to cover her breasts with one arm and the dense mat of dark hair below with her other hand. She was standing on a stack of paper covered with mathematical symbols written in blood.

ten

"WHAT HAPPENED, DADDY?"

Brad had just booted his computer and turned his phone back on when the ringtone started. "What? What's up Angie?"

"Friday morning, that's what's up. I tried to Skype you last night, but you were offline. And you didn't answer your phone. Are you okay?" There was a hint of hurt and annoyance mixed in with her concern.

"I turned everything off. I'm sorry. I just needed to get away, and . . . I can't believe I forgot what day it was."

"That's okay. I was just worried. And I wanted to tell you about the dance last weekend."

"Oh, right. How did it go? How was Kermit?"

"Kevin! He was..." She let out a single pulse of laughter. "You did warn me about older men."

"Whoa. What did this guy try? No, don't tell me. I don't want his death on my conscience. Are you all right?"

"Daddy! Of course, I'm all right. I just didn't expect to be that involved that fast."

"Involved?"

"Daddy! We just kissed. And a little ... but ..." The pause

stretched out. "I mean, he's really nice and really smart, but he is . . . determined."

"Don't let him push you into anything you're not ready for."

"You sound like a health lecture, Daddy. I've heard that one over and over. No, it's not like . . . oh, I don't know. Maybe the problem is that I actually am ready."

"What? You're sixteen. How can you be ready for . . . for anything?"

"Yes, Daddy, I'm sixteen. Mom was sixteen when she lost her virginity. To you."

"And look where it got her."

"Married to you, Daddy, and now married to her work. Well, and Adam. But that doesn't count because he's married to his work, too."

"Sounds like a good match. But we were talking about you."

"Right. I just don't know. Kevin was, well, wonderful. And I liked it. And I was really glad that he moved so fast. And why I am talking with you about this? You're my father."

"You're talking with me about this because you can. And you never could talk with your mother about these things. Not after . . ." The words were never said—not anymore—but they often filled the interstices when the talk between them got serious.

"Daddy?"

"Yes?"

"I love you."

"Me, too."

"I think I figured this one out."

"Really?"

"I'm talking with you about it. It's obvious. I'm not ready for more. If I were, I would have already . . . you know . . . done it."

"Always the one to logic it out."

"I'm your daughter."

"Lucky me."

"Look, I gotta get ready for school. Thanks for talking."

"Anytime. I have lectures to prepare, so I better go, too. Hey, next Thursday won't work either."

"I'm being replaced."

"Never. I'm lecturing late at UMass, a favor for a friend."

"Armand."

"Right. I forget you already know about Armand."

"Okay. Love you. Bye."

"Love you. Later."

◊

His cellphone on the seat beside him was ringing for the third time as Brad took the exit and turned toward the University of Massachusetts Amherst Campus. He looked down to check the caller ID. All zeros, probably some robo-dialer. He ignored it until it stopped. Only a few seconds passed before the phone started ringing again, displaying the same caller ID. This time he answered.

"Yo. Brad here."

"Where are you?" The voice was resonant, breathy, and playful. "What are you doing?"

"I am driving and shouldn't be talking on the phone with you, Ms. DeTuring. Please, I told you not to phone me."

"It's Reggi. Call me Reggi. Some kids at school call me Gina, but I want you to call me Reggi. And I'm not phoning you; I'm using MoomBeam."

"You're what? You're using a moonbeam?"

"No, silly, MoomBeam. It's like Skype but it works inside a browser, so you can use it from any computer, like even at school. Some students in India, Mumbai, wrote the software. You can call any telephone with it free. Phoebe knows how the hack works; I don't."

"Please tell me you are not calling from your school."

"Do you think I am stupid? No, I'm at Phoebe's. We're listening to music."

"You are? I don't hear any Justin Bieber squealing in the background."

"Bieber? Oh, please, no. Phoebe is into LinkinPark, that sort of thing. I prefer classical music. You don't hear anything because Phoebe has her earbuds in and I'm listening to you."

"You like classical music? Like Bach? Beethoven?"

"Oh, God, no. I meant classical, like Devo, The Smiths, Edie Brickell and the New Bohemians. I like smart songs with something to say. Phil Collins and Genesis, Tears for Fears, Denton Reynolds. You know, old stuff."

"Right, old stuff. Before you were born. The music of my youth. But who's Denton Reynolds?"

"You don't know Denton Reynolds? Singer-songwriter from Maine? 'Teachable Moments?' It's a classic. 'When the teacher becomes the student, and the classroom is the hall.' No? How old are you, anyway?"

"Old enough. Look, I need to turn into this lot and try to find a parking space. And . . . excuse me while I avoid a collision with an SUV."

Brad braked in time to avoid the black Ford Explorer, but the driver stopped alongside and lowered his window.

"You some kind of a moron? This is a parking lot! Your idiot phone conversation can wait thirty seconds until you're parked." The man rolled the window back up and continued out the exit.

Brad picked up his phone again. "Did you hear that."

"Yeah, who does that jerk think he is?"

"The Dean of Students, UMass Amherst."

"Really?"

"No, I just made that up."

The laughter on the phone made Brad smile. "I do have to hang up. I've got a lecture to give."

"Topology?"

"No, quasi-experimental design. Returning a favor for a prof who took some of my classes when I was sick last year."

"They don't just let you cancel?"

"For us part-timers, no preachy no paycheck. But this one is free and should be a pleasure."

"Oh, I guess you better go, then. Freedom and pleasure. Make the most, right?"

Brad grinned and started humming.

"There you go. Classics. Like 'Everybody Wants to Rule the World.' That's what I mean. Later." Click.

Brad shook his head in self-reproach. "You have to stop this," he said to the silent phone and to himself.

◊

The two-hour class did not start off particularly well. The nursing students, mostly young women, but with more men than Brad would have expected, were scattered around the large classroom, making it feel like lecturing to an empty hall. They asked no questions and responded to his questions with shrugs and trapped expressions. "This is going to be on your mid-term exam, so it better make sense to you," he told them, knowing that such warnings carried no weight. He leaned forward and looked straight at one student, a bored blonde with a purple streak in her hair seated alone in the front row. "Are they always this lively?" he asked. "Or are they trying to bore me with the sound of my own voice?" She shrugged and looked around, but the class laughed politely.

At the very end, he finally got them engaged when he described a hypothetical ad campaign by a drug company touting the results of one of its studies. He asked them whether they should believe the ad hype on the basis of the research, and he pushed them to criticize the experimental design.

Two students, a male and female who had been sitting together in the second row, came up to him after class and asked several questions about research ethics as he was closing his laptop and gathering his notes. They followed him to his car as they continued the conversation, asking how he knew Professor Richelieu. Brad recognized it for what it was: more curiosity about him than about the subject of the lecture.

"Armand Richelieu is just a colleague," he told them, answering the unasked question. As they walked away, huddled in private conversation, he shook his head and said quietly, "I suppose two live bodies out of twenty-nine is not too bad for an evening class."

◊

The house was dark when he got back to West Hopeland; he had forgotten to turn on the light at the top of the stairs. In the recent thawing trend the ice and snow on the roof melted during the day, dripped onto the steps, and then refroze every night, leaving a slick, invisible film of black ice. With his shoulder still reminding him of the consequences of inattention, Brad made his way slowly and deliberately up the steep stairs. He was on the landing when he heard his name called from the darkness below.

"Brad."

"Gillian?"

"Yes. Just checking on you. We missed you at Mandy's. With neither you nor Armand there, Tom never stopped talking."

"I had a class to teach in Amherst. Returning an old favor from Armand."

"Have you eaten?"

"No, no time, and I need to return Armand's car to him. He and his beau were celebrating some kind of month-a-versary or something. They flew to Quebec for dinner and an overnight. Must be nice."

"Armand's a pilot, too?"

"No, but his new boyfriend is. Flies for one of the regionals—I don't remember which—and owns a small plane. I'm supposed to drop Armand's car off at his place. The pilot left his car at the airport."

"How will you get back from Armand's?"

"Hitch, call a cab."

"Let me walk back and get my car. I'll follow you to Armand's and then we can go get something to eat."

"Okay. Let me dump my stuff first."

"It's cold. Can I come up?"

"Sure, I suppose. Let me get the light on so I don't end up getting sued when my lawyer friend slips and falls."

Inside, he turned on the porch light and the kitchen light, and gave the room a quick review. For once, there were no dirty dishes stacked in the sink, and he had remembered to take out the trash bag by the door on his way out earlier.

Gillian rattled her fingers on the glass and let herself in. "Cozy," she said, looking around.

"That's one word for it, I suppose. Minimal also comes to mind. There's no dishwasher, the kitchen sink clogs twice a month, and the drafts under the door reach gale force at times, but it's home. I've gotten real good at hand washing, I buy drain cleaner in five-gallon jugs, and I have an old towel I use as a door snake to keep the breezes at bay. For every problem, a solution. But, I am sure you know, every solution breeds a new problem, so progress is nothing but an illusion."

"Yes, but 'still it is necessary to keep struggling on toward solution.' Misquote Sheldon Kopp to me, and see where it gets you. And you, you can be so Marvin-like at times, Brad."

"It's the price of having a brain the size of a small planet. I'm not a pessimist, mind you, just a realist. Live long enough and life beats you down."

"You haven't lived long enough to be beaten down."

"Oh, I could tell you tales."

"I'm sure, but can we do it over something to eat?"

"You're really hungry."

"Starved. Famished."

"Sit down. Here." He pulled out one of the three chairs at the small kitchen table. "I'll make you something."

"Oh, no. Don't be silly, I can last another ten minutes."

"It takes longer than that just to get to Armand's. By the time we then drive someplace, order, and get served, another hour will have gone by. By then, who knows, you'll faint and then you'll sue me. So, don't you be silly. Despite appearances, I actually can cook, even though I seldom do."

"I don't know what to say. I wasn't expecting this."

"Neither was I, so the frittata I am about to conjure for you will be sui generis, made with whatever I can find in the fridge that doesn't have exotic new life forms growing on it."

◊

Brad checked his watch as he turned off the fire under the omelet pan. "There. Fourteen minutes, flat."

"You cheated. You didn't start timing until you began chopping and mixing."

"Did not."

"Did too. Oh, that does smell good."

"Really, would you like some?" he teased, waving the pan back and forth in front of her. He used the spatula to fold the frittata over in the pan, divide it in two, and slide half onto her plate and half onto his own. "There. Under fifteen minutes. Emergency rations for a starving friend."

"More like eighteen, I would say." She slipped a forkful into her mouth and raised her eyebrows. "Mmm, this is good."

"Not a second over seventeen, Counselor. I enter into evidence one digital stopwatch, which—"

"I know what you are, Bradley Williams. I just figured it out. You are manic-depressive, and now you are entering your manic phase."

"Brilliant diagnosis, Doctor Rappaport. But Sousa-2-N would disagree. She said I had a personality disorder."

"Who?"

"Uh, the shrink who worked with my daughter and me after the divorce. Her full name was Susan Charlotte Sousa, but I claim she had left off the last syllable from her middle name. Like all of her profession, she was actually a charlatan."

"That's funny, clever. You really dislike therapists."

"Not all of them, just the ones I've met. Or heard of. Or am yet to meet or hear of. They're worse than lawyers. No offense. Present company excepted, of course."

"Of course. But what turned you against an entire profession? What did they do to you?"

"Took my daughter away from me."

"Do you want to talk about it?"

"No." He took a breath and forced a smile. "How was the frittata?"

She nodded enthusiastically as she finished the last bite. "It was delicious. I am amazed at what you can cook up in eighteen minutes."

"Fourteen. Flat."

She smiled warmly at him and winked. "I'll help you clean up. Then we better get Armand's car back."

◊

Brad was the first at Mandy's the following Thursday, and Gillian was the second. He looked up as she approached, then resumed his study of the inlaid compass-rose pattern in the tabletop. She sat beside him and boldly placed her hand on top of his. "What's wrong?"

He looked down at her hand but said nothing. She spread her fingers, lifted her hand, and rested it beside his.

"They rejected my request for expanded visitation with Angie."

"Did they give a reason?"

He laughed. "Yes, oddly. They, quote, see no reason to modify the present arrangements, unquote. No reason is the reason."

"Do you want me to look into this? Family law is not my thing, but maybe I can help."

"And maybe you can't. It's my problem, anyway, and I prefer to just keep it that way. Sorry. I don't mean to be an Eeyore again."

"Marvin. Remember?"

"Right. Brain the size of a small planet." He broke into a big smile. "How do you do it? Every time I get worked into a first-class funk, you come along and make me smile. It is not fair, Counselor. Surely you have some sense of professional ethics that would hold against such manipulative interference. Leading the witness, isn't it? It's my God-given right as an American to be morose."

"Morose but not verbose."

"Oh, please don't take my loquacious ways away. Not that, too. If I am compelled to smile, can I not at least babble at the same time?"

Her hand was now atop his again, and they were grinning at each other as Armand approached. He raised one eyebrow as he tilted his head in inquiry.

"Don't do that," Brad exclaimed.

"Why?"

"Because . . . because I have never been able to do it myself." He tried to raise one eyebrow but succeeded only in a lopsided squint. "See? I can't do it. And that engenders deep and illogical envy, that's why."

"Isn't all envy illogical?"

"Not from the perspective of evolutionary logic." It was Tom

Carraway, making his deep-throated announcement as he sauntered over to join them. With that, the Coconut Club had been called to order again, and the first Topic of Today had been declared: Evolution and Envy.

eleven

HUMILIATED AND FURIOUS with herself, Reggi tried to shrivel into invisibility at her desk in the second row.

"I thought your little sister was the big brain." Aaron Pretzky, Jack's right-hand buddy, leaned over Reggi's shoulder trying to catch a glimpse down her blouse.

"She is, dumbass. Or at least she thinks she is." Jack flat-handed Aaron on the shoulder, sending him stumbling backward. Aaron faked serious injury and threw himself across the desk behind Reggi, triggering a rush of laughs among the dozen students in the classroom.

"All right, Pretzky, that will be enough." Mr. Gest, who taught math and coached lacrosse, drummed on his teacher's desk with a fat index finger. "You're here in detention for a reason. I expect you to use the time to do some work—quietly."

Detention for missing homework was a first for Reggi, an experience made all the worse by the prospect of spending an hour in the same room as Jack and his friend Aaron. For them, detention was more or less a regular event, and her presence was a welcome and hilarious distraction.

Whispers. "Hey, smart girl, can you please, please help a poor, dumb, horny boy with his homework?"

Mumbles. "I'm flunking the health and hygiene unit. Can you help me with this stuff about STDs? I need a demonstration." Laughter from the back followed by more finger drumming from the front of the room.

"Hey, Jack, what's this thing with your sister. Aren't girl geniuses all flat-chested?" More giggles. More drumming.

"Leave her alone, guys." At last a defense from one of the other girls.

The hour dragged as Reggi doodled equations in her notebook. Ironically, the missing homework, a trivial worksheet, was already finished, still sitting on the breakfast bar at home. She had been puzzling over the four-color theorem before school and had forgotten to slip the homework paper into her backpack.

She was relieved when the interminable hour finally ended, and Jack called out to his buddies. "Pizza at Pomo's, everybody." Pomodori's and the Dairy Queen farther up the street survived mainly on the after-school trade from perpetually hungry teen-agers.

Reggi was not hungry. She watched Jack and his friends saunter up the street, then turned the other way to jog home rather than wait for the late bus. She was eager to explain her new insight to Bradley. Bradley. She loved the sound of the name. Bradley from South Hadley. Except he wasn't. She was being silly and she knew it. The proof. It was time to get back to the proof.

At home, she fired up her blood-red Alienware laptop and launched Firefox, clicked on the InStarTute bookmark, and waited for the automatic login to finish. Instead of the student homepage, a message popped up. "Incorrect student ID or password. Please try again." She shut down the browser, launched it again, and got the same results. Annoyed that Firefox may have lost her passwords, she manually entered "DeTuring" and "haltin9problem." The login was rejected again with an added message to contact tech support.

Cursing under her breath, Reggi clicked on the Help button for the site and found her way to a live chat link.

Technician: How can I help you?

Student: this stupid system won't let me log in

Tecnician: Are you a regular user?

Student: yes i'm a regular user. now i just get this popup

Technician: What does the pop-up message say?

Student: tells me my ID or password is wrong

Technician: What is your student Id on this site?

Student: DeTuring

Technician: Please wait a minute while I retrieve your account record.

Technician: That account has been blocked from access. There's a flag for inapropriate communication.

Student: what the f does that mean?

Technician: I don't know. Could be that kind of language. Or socializing online with a tutor.

Student: thats bull. how do i get reinstated?"

Technician: You need to create the account again from one of your school computers, just like when you first registered.

Student: look, i need help with my homework. i'm at home, not at my school. tomorrow at school is too late

Technician: I am sorry, but that's how the system works.

Student: isn't there something you can do? hack into the thing or something

Technician: I am sorry, but there is nothing I can do.

Student: you have to do something. i have to get back into the system. please

Technician: What is your school and student number?

Student: ipswich, IHS, 20130017
Technician: And your full name?
Student: Regina Elizabeth Josephson Bellingham.
Technician: Hi, Regina. I'm Malcolm. In case we get
    disconnected.
Student: we better not. i need to get logged in
Technician: Is there any way you can prove your identity?
Student: how? you want a credit card number? i don't have a
    driver's license
Technician: A photo would do.

The request seemed strange.

Student: a photo? you want a photo of me?
Technician: Yeah, just to verify your identity.
Student: don't have a photo of me on the computer. don't see
    how that could work anyway
Technician: We have face-recognition algorithms.
Student: i told you i don't have a photo.
Technician: You could turn on your Web cam in IM mode.

Reggi looked at the tiny lens at the top of her laptop and suddenly
felt exposed. Without thinking, she put her thumb over the camera.
With her left index finger she typed her reply.

Student: just saved off a pdf copy of this chat session, which
    i am going to send to your boss, malcolm, and get you fired
    unless you reactivate my account immediately
Technician: No need to threaten. I can override the lock.
Student: then do it. and don't ever try to pull something like
    this again
Technician: Your account is reactivated. But I would
    recommend you reread the Terms of Service. Don't
    socialize with tutors and do watch your language online.

She typed, "fuck you, pervert!" but didn't press the Enter key.

Her next attempt to login succeeded and took her to the student homepage. She typed a message for TUTOR-10 but erased it. Malcolm might be watching, she told herself.

She typed a fresh IM message: "we need to get on with proving the theorem. see new version of lemma 3.14 in your dropbox."

She retyped her original message to Bradley using Notepad, saved it into a password-protected ZIP folder, and dragged the folder into TUTOR-10's dropbox before logging out. She figured that TUTOR-10 was smart enough to guess the password, and she hoped that Malcolm was not.

◊

Reggi was about to shut down for the night when the little Taj Mahal icon on her laptop started blinking to an incoming call on her MoomBeam account. It was a text message: "Okay. You win. Tomorrow night."

twelve

REGGI LET HERSELF INTO the empty split-level house on Birch Lane. On Fridays, Jack worked late at the Market Basket, and this week Big Jack was still away on a construction job in Connecticut. He would return Saturday afternoon, bellow and growl while watching television in the den until he finished his first six-pack, and then pass out on the couch with the big-screen television playing to no one.

The house was too big and too small. The finished basement held the den, the guest room that never saw a guest, the separate bath with its double shower, and the utility room. Five bedrooms and three full baths for a family of three. And it still felt crowded to Reggi when both Jacks were home at once.

With the house to herself, Reggi could spread out rather than retreat to her bedroom at the end of the hall. She pulled her laptop from her backpack and set it up on the breakfast bar. While it was booting up, she retrieved a juice box from the pantry and some cheese from the door of the fridge. With a rolled-up slice of Muenster in one hand and the Box-o-Berries in the other, she sat on one of the backless stools and waited as her computer finished connecting to the house Wi-Fi.

Big Jack was no Einstein, but he was clever with things. He had added the three-car garage to the house and renovated the basement. He had installed the Wi-Fi and debugged the repeaters by trial-and-error. He worked in the construction trades at almost anything—from plumbing and electrical to light carpentry—as long as he could get by without producing a license or a union card.

His son took after him—not stupid, but no mental giant, smart with tools but not with people, and certainly not with abstractions. To both of them, what Reggi did with her time on the Internet was a mystery, a mystery that irritated them because it put her out of their grasp.

Reggi, trying to act as if she was not in a hurry, checked Facebook and picked up her regular email before switching to her extra account. There it was: confirmation. The weekend was on! Finally. She was ready. Her big purple backpack had been packed and ready to go since yesterday. A shower and fresh clothes, and she would be long gone before Jack returned.

"What's up?"

Startled at the voice just over her shoulder, Reggi swung around, arm bent, and caught Jack in the chin with her elbow. He grabbed her arm and twisted it up her back. "Violent little bitch, as always."

"Let go of me, asshole, or . . ."

"Or what, shrimp? What is my brainy, booby little sister going to do?" He pressed her arm up higher, forcing her to lift herself from the seat. With her free arm, she reached back and hammered at Jack's crotch. He groaned in a high pitch and loosened his hold on her arm enough for her to twist away, sending the stool crashing into him.

He straightened up again, panting, to face the point of a kitchen knife in her hand. It was the big one, with the handle that didn't match the others. It felt good in her hand, good to be waving it in front of his face.

"Or I'll amputate your ugly nose," she said. "That's 'or what.' Now leave me alone."

"I'll leave you alone for now. But later, well, who knows? We can play some games, video games."

"Later? Later you can play with yourself in the shower, Jack. I'm out of here."

"Where? Does Dad know?"

She curled her lip. "Yes, Big Jack knows, and it's none of your business." She side-stepped up from the sunken kitchen area while still facing him with the knife in her hand. Then she turned and headed down the hall. The sound of her bedroom door slamming echoed in the empty house.

Jack waited several minutes, expecting to hear her emerge, but there was not a sound from the end of the hall. He walked heavy-footed to be sure she knew he was approaching. "Hey, Regina, booby ballerina. It's okay. It's all okay. Let's not fight. I've got some weed. We can do Netflix." No sound from the other side of the door. "I'm sorry. Didn't mean to scare you. We be friends again?" Nothing.

He tried the knob. To his surprise the door opened, letting a whistle of wind rush in through the crack at the bottom of the window facing the back of the house. He went over to look out, not sure what he expected to see in the muddy back lawn and dull gray of winter dusk. He slammed the window down and stomped out of her room.

◊

Jack didn't see her come back late Sunday afternoon, but Big Jack somehow sensed the moment she was home. "Where the hell you been, girl?" he boomed up the stairs from the den.

"Linda's," she answered, figuring he probably couldn't hear her above the warfare raging on the video playing in the background. "The sleep-over I told you about. You said fine."

"What? What did you say? Com'ere. Come down here so I can hear you."

She sighed and started down the stairs just as he was starting up. Beer slopped from the fresh bottle of Molson's in his left hand. He steadied himself on the railing with the other. "Shit, now look at the carpet. See what you made me do? I don't have time to clean this up. I gotta hit the road and drive down to New Jersey for another job. Would you believe they are still doing repairs and construction from that Sandy thing? How long's it been? Still haven't fixed stuff. Government. Vultures. Tightwad vultures. Bossy foremen. Sassy teenagers. I hate 'em all."

He sat down on the bottom step. "Make me some coffee. I think I need some coffee before . . ." He set his beer down a little too fast, and foam slopped over the side. "Son of a bitch. Clean this damn soggy mess up. Make me some coffee, then clean this up. Whole damn place smells like some beer-puke roadhouse."

Reggi left him at the bottom of the stairs where he sat mumbling something about mob jobs and construction bonuses. She started the electric kettle without bothering to check the water level, spooned some instant coffee into a striped mug, and looked around for an extra towel. The teakettle clicked off with a scant few tablespoons of water boiling away at the bottom. Reggi ran some tap water into the kettle and clicked it back on.

When it came to food, Big Jack had all the taste of a plastic pelican—like the bright pink one beside the driveway outside. The only thing he wanted from coffee was that it was hot and black. He snacked on Tex-Mex tortilla chips dusted with mysterious red-orange powder, ate cheese sandwiches made with white bread and processed cheese, and called a bacon-double-cheeseburger smothered with onions and mustard a gourmet feast. His one affectation was his beer. His buddies all drank Bud Lite, but he swilled nothing but Molson's ever since a Canadian carpenter had grabbed his tool belt to keep him from sliding off a roof job in northern New Hampshire. They had toasted at the end of the day with a Molson's—sweet piss from the North Country, the man had called it, grinning at the sincerest of roughneck compliments for a favorite brew.

Reggi finished with the spill, tossed the beer-soaked towel in the laundry room, and climbed the stairs. Big Jack was loudly slurping his coffee and complaining that it was too hot. "Put some cold water in it if it's too hot," she said, reaching for the mug.

"Don't be stupid. Dilute it? I need this. Gotta drive through the fuckin' night and meet this damn crew at five fuckin' ay-em."

Reggi knew better than to argue, but she worried whenever he took off like this. If something happened to Big Jack, she'd be alone with Jack. They'd probably make him her guardian. Ha. Some guardian. She worried just as much about something happening to Jack. She was better off with both of them. Domestic détente.

"Fix a thermos of coffee for me, Sweetie. I'm going to grab my duffle and go."

Sweetie. He could seem so, so nice when he wanted something. Jack, too. Like father, like son. Two of a kind.

She watched as Big Jack roared his dirty blue 4-by-4 down the driveway, then went to her room and locked the door. She was not as handy with tools as Big Jack, but she was better than her all-thumbs stepbrother. She slid the newly installed deadbolt in place and hoped Jack would stay stoned for a few more hours.

◊

It was much the same story the following week. "This, young lady, is the third weekend in a row," Big Jack bellowed as he staggered up the stairs. "What the hell do you two do at Linda's house?"

"Study. Talk. Stuff."

"Study, huh. That super math shit, I suppose. Is she as big a geek as you?"

"Bigger. So can I go now?"

"What am I going to do? Who's going to make my coffee and eggs in the morning?"

"The cooks at Mickey-D's, as always. I never make you breakfast and don't intend to start this weekend."

"Come here, Sweetie. We don't have to fight before you go." He reached out and hooked an arm around her waist before she could dance beyond his reach.

"We don't have to fight afterwards, either." She squirmed in his grip. "You and Jack will be just fine without me. It's only a weekend."

"Another weekend." He let his hand slip down from her waist. "Such a cute ass."

She slapped his hand away and pulled free. "And a big mouth. Talks all the time, never stops. Remember."

"Now, Sweetie, we don't have to get all in a huff." He put his hands on top of his head. "This Linda, do I know her? Where does she live? In town? Need a ride?"

"No, we're meeting at Pomo's, then her mom's picking us up. The number's on the list by the phone. I'll be back Sunday evening. Don't wait up." There was no Linda on the list, but she knew Big Jack would never go so far as to actually check.

◊

Reggi's heart was pounding as she rounded the corner, cut through the Bruce's wide driveway, and doubled back. She had made up her mind. This was the weekend. It was time.

She was too caught up in her thoughts to notice who was following her.

thirteen

ARMAND TOOK ANOTHER SIP of his mochachino. "And how are things going with your little math-whiz Lolita?"

"Lolita was twelve. This girl is a senior in high school, nearly an adult."

"And you are no Humbert Humbert, we would assume. Or hope. But what is it about this girl that has you hypnotized?"

"She is fascinating."

"Interesting choice of words."

"She has this machine-gun way of attacking mathematical problems. She often moves so fast I have to ask her to slow down for me. She has an eidetic memory for music as well as math, and can repeat the lyrics of almost any song. She even introduced me to a singer-songwriter named Denton Reynolds—quoted him verbatim. Ever hear of him?"

"Yeah. Heard him perform live once. He opened at some folk-rock festival out this way not long before he offed himself."

"Well, I never heard of him. I had to track his stuff down on the Internet. There's a YouTube video from a gig he did at Passim in Cambridge. His one-and-only album, 'Teachable Moments,' is out-of-print but on offer on eBay."

"You really didn't know Denton Reynolds? And you claim to be a New England native. You led a sheltered life, my friend." Armand started singing in his gravelly baritone:

> When the teacher becomes the student
> And the classroom is the hall,
> Then the teachings of philosophy
> Are rewritten on the wall.

He belted out the chorus.

> Teach, that you may learn again,
> And learn, that you might teach me.
> In the answers of your questioning,
> May your someday wisdom reach me.

"Surely, you've heard that."

"I have—twice: in an MP3 track online and now in your . . . funkier rendition."

Armand took a twisting, comic bow. "So, what does she look like, this wunderkind of yours?"

"Dark, wavy hair, a dimpled face, deep brown-black eyes that . . . I . . ."

"Exactly. You are so over your head here, my friend. You need to turn around before you are too far from shore to swim back."

"It's not what you think. She comes from this poor, messed up family, and with some proper mentoring—"

"Proper. Emphasis on that word, Bradley Williams."

"It is not what you think."

"Then tell me what I think. No, don't. We'll start into one of those damn recursions where you are saying what you think I think that you think or some such nonsense. Truth be told, I don't care about what might be going on. I'm not one to talk, anyway. But I do care about you. I don't want to have to come visit you in an institution for sex offenders."

"You won't. Nothing is going to happen except I am going to help a young genius turn the math world upside down."

"As long as you don't turn her upside down." Armand spread his hands. "Or whatever turns you on."

"The reason you can think I might take advantage of this girl is that you can never stop thinking about sex."

Armand saluted. "Guilty as charged, sir. Along with half the human race: the male half. Actually three-quarters of the human race. And a hundred percent of the human race under twenty-five."

"You are a true cynic, Armand. And a pervert."

"Pervert, yes, but cynic, no. Optimist. Incurable. Love is always possible, everywhere, anytime. And the rest of the time, a good roll in the hay will do just fine. Who knows, I might even be persuaded to switch hit again by the right teen queen with a big vocabulary and the tits to match. Maybe someone deep, like your Linda Lovelace. No, that was the other one. I mean Ada Lovelace, of course."

"How is it that the refined intellectual we see on Thursdays at Mandy's can be so crude when it's just the two of us?"

"That's how. Think about it."

◊

Jenna was loading something in her car when Brad came walking up the street. "Well, look who's here? And how are you doing, Bradley, on this beautiful spring-like day?"

Brad crossed the street on impulse. "I'm good. Need a hand?"

"No, I'm done. Donations for the Good Shepherd rummage sale. I've been collecting. And, yes, you are good, Bradley, a good man, even if you are given to coarse language and poor grammar. But I know that you meant to say that you are well, doing well."

So, he was thinking, you're a grammar evangelist, too. He

shrugged. "I'm good and well, then. Both."

"Where have you been? We've hardly seen you lately." She picked up her dog from where it had been dozing on the front seat. "Yvette and I have missed you."

"Really. Both of you? Well, I've been busy. Teaching. Tutoring. Using coarse, ungrammatical language. Just kidding. It's that time of year when homework piles up. You know."

"Oh, how well I know. I teach Sunday School at the Good Shepherd. You have to study to teach. That is maybe the best part of teaching. You know, you really should come to services sometime. You would love Pastor Barbara. She is so inspiring. It's across town, but I would be more than glad to drive you there some Sunday."

"Is Yvette a church-goer, too?"

Jenna blinked, flashed a frown, then restored her smile of tolerance. "You are a tease, Bradley."

"That I am. And a busy one. My weekends are never my own anymore. You two will just have to praise the Lord without me. For me."

"Oh, I will do that, Bradley. You know, I pray for you."

He wanted to say, I'll bet you do, but he nodded his thanks and turned to cross the street. At the driveway he heard a sharp yap and the squeal of tires behind him. Turning, acting on impulse, Brad took two long strides, scooped up Yvette in his big hands, and continued across the street just as one of the Mackenzie brothers swerved, skidded, and raced on down the block in his red Mustang.

"Oh, my. My God! Oh, my goodness." A shaken Jenna took Yvette from Brad and began to smother the squirming dog in kisses. She turned her face to the sky and closed her eyes. "Thank you, Lord, thank you for saving Yvette." Brad stood, blinking, catching his breath. "And you, Bradley, you, too. Who would know that you would become the instrument of God's love for his small creatures."

Brad opened his mouth to respond but said nothing. He half turned to start again across the now quiet street with its freshly carved black skid marks.

"You take care of yourself, Bradley, you dear man."

"I will do that. And you, too, Jenna," he said over his shoulder. When he reached the top of the stairs, he glanced back. She was still standing there, holding her dog, watching him.

fourteen

NEW-STEM, THE REGIONAL SCIENCE, Technology, Engineering, and Mathematics teachers' conference in New Haven the following month, was a welcome distraction that let Brad escape his demons and the drag of classes for a few days. To his surprise, he was able to convince the college to subsidize his attendance. He had arranged to borrow Armand's car for the drive to and from Connecticut. Virgil Sandborg, an overweight engineer-turned-teacher from the middle-school, was going to share the driving on the way down but was planning to stay over with relatives afterwards, leaving Brad on his own for the return. Brad already knew Virgil on account of occasional drop-in appearances at the Muffin and Mug. They were both looking forward to the trip, the change of scene, and opportunities to network with other STEM teachers in the region.

◊

Brad had collapsed on returning home from the conference late on Sunday and had spent most of Monday recovering. It was already Tuesday evening before he finally got around to finishing unpacking. He was sorting notes from the trip when there was a knock. He turned on the light and opened the inner door. Through the storm door he could see two men; the closer one was holding up a badge. "Police. I'm Lieutenant Lefkowitz and this is Detective Sergeant Hamilton. Are you Bradley Williams?" Brad nodded twice. "We'd like to talk with you. May we come in?"

Brad did not reach for the handle immediately. "What's this about?"

"We'd just like to ask you some questions. May we come in?"

"Am I under arrest or anything?"

"No, we just want to ask some questions. May we come in?"

Brad's mind raced. He could insist on a warrant, but that was likely only to worsen the matter. What did they know? Play it cool, he told himself.

"Sure, I suppose. Come on in. Please excuse the mess. Here, we can sit at the table." He pushed aside the conference papers he had been sorting. "So, what is this about?"

"Do you know anything about a Web service called InStarTute?"

"I do. I'm a tutor on that site."

"Do you know a student named Regina Elizabeth Bellingham?"

"We don't have access to student names. We only know them by their screen names, their handles."

"Okay, then, do you know a student who used the handle DeTuring?"

"Yes, I have done some online tutoring with that student, the one who uses that handle, but the terms of service don't allow social contact between tutors and student clients." He was choosing his words with care, making everything a truth. No lies. Don't get caught in a lie.

"So then, you wouldn't know her current whereabouts, would you?"

"No, I don't know her whereabouts. I told you, the only way tutors are allowed to know their students is through their screen names. We can communicate with their schools if the need arises."

"What sort of a need might that be?"

"Well, like if we suspect they are in trouble or something."

"I thought you weren't allowed casual communication."

"We aren't, but these are kids, teenagers. They look at rules differently than you and I do. And it might be something as simple as falling behind in a class or something. That sort of thing. Why? Is this . . . this kid in trouble?"

"No. She's not in trouble. At least we hope not. She's missing. Her father thinks she ran away. When the local police asked about online activity, he said she used that website. We confirmed it. Her father remembered her talking about tutor number ten. That's you, as we found out. And here we are? When was the last contact you had with her?"

Brad tensed, fighting to control his shaking. "Sorry about how cold this place is. I just got back from a conference in New Haven, and the apartment takes forever to warm up." He shivered. "What were you asking?"

"When was your last contact with the Bellingham girl?"

"Let's see. Last contact—via the website, of course—would have been just over a week ago, before I left for the conference. I am sure you can check the website logs."

"I am sure we can. Nothing since? Okay, you give us a call if you hear from her or anything. Don't try to handle things yourself. Call us. We just want to get her home safe."

"Yes, of course. Home. Safe. I'll do that. I'll call if anything . . . I'll call."

It seemed to take them forever to put on their coats, pick up their gloves, and take their leave. All the time, their eyes darted about, inspecting, taking everything in. Brad's heart was pounding so hard that he was sure they could hear it.

"Goodnight, Mr. Williams. We'll be in touch if we need anything more from you."

"Right. Anytime. Anything."

"And don't worry. Kids run away, and most of the time they just show up again, and that's it. She'll probably be back any day now."

"How long has it been?"

"Several days. But she still could turn up at some boyfriend's house or something. He'd be the one in deep trouble. Harboring's not a joking matter. Runaways? That's a different story. I wouldn't want to risk harboring. Especially an adult with a minor. I hope she wasn't involved with, like, a perv or anything."

"No, I hope she's all right, too."

"Well, then, Mr. Williams, that's good. Good for you." He reached out and put a hand on Brad's shoulder, giving it a squeeze that was harder than expected. "Okay, Detective, let's head in and write up our report. Thanks again, Mr. Williams. Stay warm. I hope you sleep well." He herded the Detective out, paused and looked back at Brad, then closed the door behind them.

Brad stood, unmoving, until he heard them reach the bottom of the steps, then he sat down on the kitchen floor, cross-legged, and shook.

◊

On his way to the store the next morning, Jenna pulled over to offer him a ride. He eyed the dog perched on the passenger seat. "Thanks. But I like the exercise."

She left the window down and did not pull away. "So, Bradley, what was all that about last night?"

"All what?"

"Those men. They're not local."

"Oh, those guys. No, South Hadley. They just wanted to ask some questions. No biggy."

"Questions?" She wasn't letting it go.

"Some student. Nothing. Look, I need to pick up some coffee. Gotta have my fix, you know."

"Oh, I do know. I am that way about reading the Bible. If I miss a day, I get this craving, a need for spiritual renewal."

A craving, you say. "Yeah, I guess it's a lot like that." He started to edge away.

"They looked like police, you know. That's why I was concerned. I certainly hope you aren't in any sort of trouble. If you ever want to talk, you know you can always talk with me. Okay? Remember that. God hates the sin but loves the sinner. Whatever you may have done, God's forgiveness is infinite."

"Infinite. Right. Okay, see you." He waved as walked away.

◊

After the next meeting of the Coconut Club, Brad pulled Gillian aside. "I need to talk with you. In private."

"What's up?"

"Take a walk with me, and put on your attorney's hat." As he walked her to her car, he told her a condensed version of the interrogation.

"They were fishing," she said, "not very sophisticated fishing, either. They were just trying to rattle you in case you knew anything. Do you?"

"No. The knock on my door was the first I knew anything might have happened with . . . the girl."

"Is there anything you haven't told me?"

"There's a million things I haven't told you. We're friends, but barely. Remember? I never told you about the time I jumped Barry Winthrop from behind in middle-school, then lied and said it was somebody else who pushed his face in the mud. I never told you I really don't like strawberries, I—"

"Okay, cut it out. You know what I meant. Is there anything about this girl?"

"Are you my attorney?"

"I told you before, I don't handle criminal cases."

"What about panic cases, I-don't-know-what's-happening cases, I'm-freaked-out-of-my-gourd cases? Do you do those? For a friend? Or a barely friend?"

She stopped, turned, and faced him squarely. "You really are scared, aren't you? And you need to talk with someone. Okay."

"Okay?"

"I'm your lawyer. You can drop by my office later and put down a token retainer. This is not my area, so I can't really help you, but this is all now privileged communication. Now, tell me what is going on? Why are you so scared? Did you have anything to do with this girl's disappearance?"

"No. Nothing. But I have, well, a record. Except not really."

"A record? But not a record?"

Brad leaned up against a parked car in the bank lot and composed his thoughts, trying to pick a starting point. "I was charged, but the charges were dropped. In the divorce. Indecent assault of a minor. My daughter." He looked at her face as she took a step back. "No, no, you don't understand. Nothing happened, nothing. It was . . . part of the craziness, something erupting from Grace's hysteria. Angie, my daughter, went along because she needed to go along, because she needed her mother more than she needed her father right then, and she so wanted to be on Grace's good side. She would have said anything."

Gillian was shaking her head, but Brad continued. "She was not quite nine. She didn't even know what she was talking about, just repeating words. And then, suddenly, she couldn't see me anymore, and I was facing jail time. That was when she realized it was no backyard game with choosing up sides, it was not about pleasing someone. So she recanted, changed her story. Except, that is not how the system works: charges by a minor they believe, admissions of false testimony they discount. But my Angie is one tough, smart, determined girl. She kept repeating the story, never wavering, never relenting, always with all the same details of how she lied and why she lied. Eventually the charges were dropped. Dropped.

"But there is still a record. There are still police files, still court-room transcripts. I was spared the life sentence the Commonwealth metes out to convicted sex offenders, but I am still condemned. That's why I can't teach in the public schools or get a regular faculty position. I can't pass the CORI; a routine background check on me turns up all this shit, this bogus shit, and that's it: no hire and leave the community, because word will get around. I did nothing, and I will pay for it the rest of my life."

"I see," she said, gravely.

"Do you? You know, something is screwy. You can go out and kill a kid on the street in a drive-by, do your time, pay your 'debt to society,' and it's over. But if you expose yourself to some kid, you are a sex offender, and for the rest of your life you will be required to register and have your name and address publicized wherever you go, and you will not be allowed to live within 500 yards of a school or church or other establishment where minors congregate. For the rest of your life. Second-degree murder and you do ten, maybe fifteen years; a sex offense, even a minor one, is a life sentence. Does that make sense? What does this say about what our society cares about, what it values?"

Gillian took in a breath, as if preparing to respond to the rhetorical question, but Brad continued. "Hell, the same perverse priorities are everywhere. The movies, television, the Internet. You can disembowel someone on camera and still get a PG-13 rating but not fondle a breast. You can show a firing squad complete with spurts of simulated blood and the death throes of actors with hoods over their heads, but a bit of tit on network primetime and society panics.

"Sorry. I'm through ranting. I'll step down from the pulpit. The summation is that I am tainted. I can't have the spotlight of suspicion turned my way, because they will go after me like hounds after a wounded fox."

"I think I understand," she said, her voice barely above a whisper. "But you didn't do anything with this girl, right? And right now they are just questioning people. You're not even a person of interest, or they would have taken you in for questioning. I think you are okay. Just stay calm and try not to worry."

"Hah. Easy for you to say. I have an advanced degree in worrying."

Gillian looked down at her boots, then back up at Brad. "I owe you an apology." He cocked his head and waited. "I thought you didn't visit your daughter because you were the typical distant dad who just didn't have time in his new life for his own kids."

Brad sighed and hung his head. "Time? I have nothing but time. I live alone in a two-and-a-half room apartment. I teach one class at Smith that meets three hours a week. I spend Thursdays from four to six at Mandy's pretending to know something. Weekends, I tutor math students online.

"If I could, I would visit Angie every weekend. But I am allowed only supervised visits and no more than once a month. Do you know what that means? Supervised? We meet in an office, an office with a goddamned social worker sitting in the corner, making sure I don't say anything 'inappropriate'—what a great, catch-all word that one is—or engage in behaviors that might be misinterpreted. I put my hand on Angie's knee once, and the damned social-work nanny coughed her disapproval. No, I would rather teleconference, except that her mother, the ever gracious, ever loving Grace, says video conferencing is too much like an unsupervised visit."

He turned away, then back again. "Shit. I don't mean to cry in my beer. And I don't even have a beer."

"We should fix that."

"Yeah, we should. You want to go to Angelo's and do bar food for a change? One of his macho nacho platters is a complete meal: chips piled with beans, jalapeños, tomatillos, slathered with sour cream, guacamole, a complete mess. You ever try that?"

"No, but I'm willing to try as long as I don't have to work."

"Work? What do you mean?"

"Can I not be your lawyer for the rest of the evening? Can we just drink and eat and be friends?"

◊

The long weekend stretched out like a dull lecture. Brad was not sure what he was most worried about. When the police showed up again on Monday, he had brief mental flashes of himself making a break out the back, but he had no car and no place to run to, so he opened the door and let them in.

"Just a few more questions, if you don't mind."

"No, sure, shoot. What do you want to know?"

"We understand that you did not have access to personal information, but did the Bellingham girl ever say anything that set off alarm bells? Was there a boyfriend maybe? Or was she in trouble."

"No, neither. Not that I knew of."

"Did she ever mention anyone else? A friend she hung out with, a teacher, anyone. Neighbors? A relative?"

"Her brother, Jack. She did mention him once. I don't think they are very close or affectionate." Brad realized there was no sense being coy; they would have access to the website logs. "And there were some online friends that she met in the chat room of the site. GeekGirl13, MODler, somebody else I can't remember; the log files from the website operator could supply that along with everyone's identity. Is there any news?"

"No. Somebody saw a girl who fit her description board a bus for

Schenectady, but we have heard nothing from the Schenectady police. She could be in California by now. Kids this age have a way of taking off and disappearing, sometimes for quite a while. I wouldn't worry."

I would, he thought. I can worry circles around the two of you. "Yeah. I just hope the kid is okay."

"So do we. Thanks for the help, Professor."

"You're welcome, Lieutenant."

◊

She was not okay, of course. They found the body three days later thanks to a tip from an off-roader following a power-line clearing. Brad read the headlines in the local paper: "Missing Teen's Mutilated Body Found West of Town." Devastated, he sank to the floor. As he read on, he could not keep from retching, and after losing his dinner of left-over pizza, he waited in dread, depressed and shaking in the cold, darkening apartment.

part two: persuasion

fifteen

"SO, WHAT HAVE WE GOT?"

Bud Hamilton grunted. "A mess, a bloody mess. Have you looked at the crime scene pictures?" He stirred his coffee, trying to get the lumps of creamer to dissolve.

Ed Lefkowitz stood in front of the cork board, staring at the posted notices without seeing any of them. "Yeah. I almost lost my breakfast."

"I've been doing this for twenty years, Ed, and never saw anything as bad as this. We have some real sicko out there."

"Or somebody really desperate to destroy the evidence. We can presume she was raped, but the medical examiner says it could be hard to prove. They're working on it."

"Okay, so who's on our shortlist?" Hamilton added an extra scoop of creamer and a splash more coffee, bringing the ecru scum to the very edge of his mug.

"This local professor, first." Lefkowitz brushed at a bushy eyebrow that threatened to overwhelm his face. "Then there's the stepfather. Seems unlikely, and he was the one who reported her missing. The stepbrother? Even more unlikely. He's what, eighteen? No car. The body was found all the way out here. Just doesn't follow, but, of course, they are not crossed off yet."

"It could also be a stranger assault, someone from completely out of left field, possibly even a serial offender."

Lefkowitz exhaled slowly. "Yeah. Possibility of last resort. Except this one doesn't fit any MO in the system, and there's nothing recent that would suggest we have a repeater to deal with. We're interviewing friends and acquaintances from her home town, of course, but right now, I'm placing my money on the professor. He's the one with a record. And remember, I told you that something didn't smell right the first time we talked with him. Too careful. Picking his words."

"He's a professor, all right." Hamilton took a sip of his coffee and scowled. "Was she kidnapped, you think?"

"Let's hope not. Then the feds take over, and we are nothing more than errand boys at best. For the same reason, let's hope nobody crossed state lines with her. I want to catch this guy. I want us to catch this guy. The body was dumped in our backyard. We don't know yet, but I'd guess the girl was killed somewhere near where they found her body. We just have to keep working, picking away at it. Take our time but not waste time. Anyone who could do this could do it again."

"What should we do about this professor dude?"

"Let's lean on him a little, keep him off balance. Maybe he'll slip and say something."

"We can bring him in for questioning as a person of interest."

Lefkowitz smiled. "Person of interest. What a lovely euphemism. Nobody knows what the hell it means. So handy."

◊

"Yes?" The voice was murky, like someone who might have just awakened from a nap.

"It's me. You're my one call, Gillian."

"What? Is this Brad?"

"This is Brad. I'm at the police station in South Hadley. They give you one call."

Gillian was suddenly very awake. "Don't say anything. Not a word until I get there. You have a right to remain silent."

"I know. Now I'm a person of interest."

"Hang on. I'll be there. Twenty minutes. Don't talk."

◊

The Brad who greeted her seemed to have shrunk. "What's going to happen?" he asked, his voice subdued, almost lost even in the small interrogation room. Under the fluorescents and with the gray walls behind him, all color was drained from him.

"They are going to ask you questions. You don't have to answer. Or you can. I'll tell you if I think you should or shouldn't answer. You should take my advice, in either case. Okay?"

Brad put his hands over his eyes and moved his chin up and down almost imperceptibly.

The door to the room opened and the two men who had picked him up at the apartment entered.

Hamilton stood by the door, and Lieutenant Lefkowitz started talking even as he seated himself across the table from Brad and Gillian. "So, is there anything more you want to tell us about your relationship with this girl, Regina Bellingham?"

"I didn't have a relationship. I provided tutoring via a website. To someone who used the handle DeTuring."

"Yeah, yeah. But you knew who she was."

Gillian put her hand on Brad's arm, but he spoke before she could say anything. "Yes, I knew her name."

"And how did you know that?"

"She called me."

"She called you? She called you, not the other way around?"

99

"Right. I never called her. She called me."

"And how did this come about, that this teenage girl from the other end of the state called you? How would she know who you were or your telephone number?"

"She was ... very smart. She got her friends to help with some online detective work. Hacking. Maybe you should consider some new recruiting strategies."

"Meaning?"

"Nothing. They were smart kids. They tracked me down."

"And then what?"

"I told her not to call me again. That was that."

"No more phone calls?"

"No, no more phone calls."

"You know, we can subpoena phone records to check this."

"Of course. I hope you do. The records will corroborate what I am telling you. She telephoned me once. I never telephoned her. I was her tutor, online. I helped her with some mathematics she was working on."

"Schoolwork?"

"Not really. She was working on a proof for a very difficult mathematical puzzle. That's what I was helping her with."

"Why did she call you?"

"That's why."

Hamilton took a step from where he was leaning against the door jamb. "What's that supposed to mean?"

"She wanted more help, more time working together."

"And?"

"And what?"

"What did you do about that?"

"I told her no."

"You didn't agree to meet with her?"

As Brad composed his thoughts, Gillian spoke up. "My client

doesn't have to answer. If you don't have any more specific questions, I would say we are finished here."

Lefkowitz eyed her with amusement. "You're not a criminal lawyer, are you, Ms. Rappaport? We'll let you know when we are finished."

"If you are not prepared to charge my client, you can't keep him."

"Forty-eight hours, Ms. Rappaport."

"I know the law, Lieutenant, and I've worked with guys like you. Hold him for questioning, place him under arrest, or let him go. You have nothing, and you are going to get nothing. There is nothing there."

"Well, as it turns out, we do have a few more specific questions. So, we'll continue for now. Tell me, Mr. Williams, where were you on the first weekend of March?"

Brad frowned in concentration. "March, first weekend, let's see. Oh, yes, I was in Connecticut, New Haven, at a conference."

"On the weekend."

"Yes, it was a teachers' conference, science and math. I stayed through the weekend, with . . . friends."

"And you can prove that."

"Yes, I believe I can. Yes. I can prove it."

Gillian stood. "Whatever the significance of those dates, my client has an alibi, so I think we are through here." She slid her chair back from the table. "Mr. Williams, do you need a ride?"

Brad was not sure what to do, but Gillian had clearly taken charge. He stood to leave.

Hamilton opened the door for them, but Lefkowitz didn't rise. He spoke to them over his shoulder. "Stay where we can reach you, Mr. Williams. We may need your help again."

◊

On the short drive back to West Hopeland, Gillian started lecturing.

"A hand on the arm ought to be enough get you to shut up. I tried to let you know not to answer. Why did you give them that bit about the phone calls?"

"Because it was all true and could be easily checked by them. If I didn't answer, they would have found out anyway from the phone records, and it would have looked much worse. Just building credibility, that's all I was doing."

"You think like a lawyer." She gave him a teasing poke. "Or a criminal mastermind."

"No, just like a mathematician, putting together a convincing proof. You build from what you have, put things in the right order. Then in the end, *quod est demonstrandum*. That's Latin. It—"

"I know. That which was to be proved. Latin. I'm a lawyer, remember? Only Catholic priests and Roman archeologists use more Latin than we do."

"We did get one thing that hasn't made the papers yet. We know when they think she was killed."

"Do you really have an alibi?"

"Really."

"You better. And you better be ready to prove it."

He shifted in his seat to get a better look at her and noticed she was smiling. "You had fun, didn't you."

"Fun is not quite the right word, but it was . . . engaging, an interesting exercise using what I know from working the other side of the table. Maneuvering. Positioning. Posturing. But I wouldn't go back to it. I can get much the same kick from real-estate law without the nerves and the heartache of criminal law."

"You're not done yet, counselor. Those two are bloodhounds, and they are going to keep dogging me."

"Probably true, which is why you are going to need a real lawyer if this goes much further. Better start looking around."

◊

He waved to Jenna as Gillian drove away. "Hey, neighbor." She turned away without answering. Well, so much for that doomed relationship, Brad was thinking as he climbed the stairs to his apartment. What next?

sixteen

"BRADLEY WILLIAMS, you have such a knack for picking the most inconvenient times to call me." She used the belt of her terrycloth robe to wipe bath bubbles off her cellphone and hoped that the seals had held against the moisture.

"They took my computer. And a bunch of stuff from the apartment."

"They?"

"The police. They had a search warrant."

"Okay, don't panic. There wasn't anything on the computer, was there?"

"Only my life and livelihood. It's going to be damn hard to keep up with teaching and tutoring without a laptop. All my notes and slides were there. My passwords. Everything."

"Not what I meant. To be blunt, was there anything that might be incriminating?"

"Maybe some things that could give the appearance."

"Some things? We better meet in my office. Give me an hour. Can you walk there or should I pick you up?

"I'll meet you there."

◊

Gillian's office on Main Street matched her personal dress code: neat, understated, stylish. She unlocked an outer office that was furnished with a light-oak receptionist's desk and matching low horizontal files. The door to a small conference room was open to the right, and straight ahead, an engraved bronze plaque marked Gillian's office. She opened the door and gestured. "Let's meet in here."

The office was larger than the conference room, with space for a desk with a return, a small round conference table, and more matching horizontal files around the perimeter. Gillian pulled out the lower drawer of one of them and extracted a folder.

Brad craned to see the contents as she opened it on the conference table. "So, I even have a file now."

"I'm a lawyer. We do files and folders for breakfast and dessert. So, fill me in on as much as you can about the contents of your computer. Anything connected with this girl?"

"Yes."

Gillian straightened her back and her voice deepened slightly as she shifted into full professional mode. "Before we go any further, I need to tell you that I want you to be completely honest with me, but there are limits. I do not want to know if you had anything to do with this girl's death. I do not want to know it. Not as your lawyer and certainly not as your . . ." She stopped, caught by the implications that were only now beginning to fully sink in.

Brad looked her in the eyes. "I didn't kill her. I don't know anything about what happened to her except what little I've read in the papers and what you and I have surmised from our encounter with the police. There were things on my computer that might look bad . . . well . . . could be interpreted . . . misinterpreted as implicating me."

"How bad?"

"Depends. There were the files relating to the mathematical proof I was helping her with. The browser history will show sites that I visited. Nothing much there. I'm really pretty straight arrow: no porn, no bomb-making plans, no celebrity stalking. I had a picture of her, though. A newspaper clipping. It might look like I was stalking her."

"And were you?"

"I did stretch the rules of the tutoring website out of curiosity about this math whiz. I didn't know she was a girl at the time. Let's leave it there."

"Okay, let's leave it there. That will not look good, but it is nothing much in itself. And what about the phone records? Were you telling the truth yesterday? Is anything else going to come back to bite?"

"No, not that I know of. If they get into the records of the tutoring site, it could look worse. There were occasional asides of a personal nature, technically off limits but nothing they could jail me for. And there were her pleas to meet and work together."

"And?"

"I always told her no, out of the question."

Gillian stood up and paced in the space between the table and her desk. "Okay. We'll just have to wait it out until their next move. In the meantime, get yourself a real lawyer, just in case."

"Just in case." He got up to leave.

"Oh, one more thing. You said they took other stuff from your apartment."

"Yeah, my brief case—that's going to be tough on me, too—and some weird stuff, like cleaning supplies from under my sink."

seventeen

JASON HARTWELL USHERED the two policemen into his office. File
storage boxes were stacked in slightly skewed towers leaving barely
enough room for the desk and a couple of armless chairs. The room
was a studied presentation of the kind of hands-on, no-pretensions
district attorney Hartwell wanted to be, but his career was stalled
behind a mixed record and a string of unimpressive cases. "Grab
another chair from the hall, Detective, and then you two bring me
up to date. Give me the Sunday supplement rundown on what we
have."

"I think we've got him."

"Bold assertion, Lieutenant. Can you put him at the scene of the
crime?"

"Maybe. Because of the thaw and rain after, we got nothing usable
in the way of footprints or tracks near the body. We do have a
rollerball pen found at the scene that matches one found in his
apartment."

"Prints?"

"Only partials, nothing definitive. But we have telephone records,
laptop files, computer server logs, chemical forensics. Looks like this
guy was stalking her, involved. And he has a record. He's a sex of-

fender. Right from the get-go, I had the sense he was our man. It's beginning to look like he lured this girl, probably raped her, then killed her and mutilated her body."

"You said probably, probably raped her. You mean you don't have semen? DNA?"

"Not exactly. Whoever did this was remarkably successful at destroying evidence."

"How is that possible?"

"Take a look at the crime scene photos and the coroner's report."

Hartwell opened the folder. "My God! What the . . .?"

"Read the report. This guy is a real sicko but a smart sicko. Fits our suspect perfect. He wiggled out of a conviction once before. Not again. We need to put him away, permanently."

Hartwell closed the folder with its disturbing photos and set his reading glasses on top of it. "Without putting him at the scene or finding the weapon or DNA evidence, a conviction is not going to be a foregone conclusion. From what you've given me, it's all circumstantial. But, I will study the file and see if we have enough to take it to a grand jury."

"Don't take your time. Just knowing this guy is still out there gives me nightmares. And, get this, he teaches at Smith College."

"Really?"

"Really. Has a small class of girls there."

Harwell scratched his chin. "Let me think about that. You keep working, talk to neighbors, all the usual shoe-leather stuff. Keep me informed while I worry about the grand jury. Close the door on your way out."

Alone again, Hartwell leafed through the folder. It was the kind of case that could launch him from the Hampshire County DA's office into a higher orbit. All he had to do was win it.

◊

Brad was blindsided by the meeting.

"I assume you've seen the papers." The HR Director had a mustache as thick and neat as Brad's was thin and untamed.

"No, I just arrived when I got your message, Perry. I was working on my notes for today's seminar. I had to . . . to regenerate some of the material."

"Well, be that as it may, Mr. Williams, you have been identified as a, quote-unquote, person of interest in a criminal case. The college has a human resources policy and procedure in place covering such situations. Where the welfare of students might be at stake, as it has been agreed applies in this case in view of the nature of the police investigation, we are required to immediately suspend or terminate the person so named."

"I didn't do anything, Perry."

"Do understand, this is not a prejudgment of guilt nor is it in any form a violation of your legal rights. It—"

"As if the assertion makes it so."

"To continue. It is merely a matter of policy and the terms of the contract you signed with the college and under which your services were retained. As you are not an employee, there will, of course, not be any need for further compensation. The contract is simply terminated without prejudice as of," he glanced at his watch, "five o'clock tonight."

Brad did not move from his chair.

"I have asked Mr. Collins here to escort you off campus." Jake Collins appeared in the open door to the office, standing in what might be interpreted as parade rest: stiffly, feet apart, hands clasped behind his back. "If you have any material in your possession belonging to the college, you are required to surrender it now. This includes," he looked down and started reading from a document, "any papers, journals, books or other publications, copies or originals, obtained from or through the library system of the college, as well as any material bearing the name or otherwise identifying any student of the college, plus—"

"Enough, Perry. The only thing I have with me are the last round of marked homework assignments for my class." He pulled the papers from the pasteboard portfolio he was using as a briefcase and slapped them down on the desk. "I also have a borrowed laptop with my notes for today's session, but, as it is not mine, it has nothing else related to the college. And you can call me Brad; we've known each other since before I started teaching here."

He turned around to face Jake Collins. "And you do not have to escort me from campus, Jake. In any case, I presume this means you won't be giving me a lift home today."

"I'm sorry, Brad, I . . ."

Perry Schuster cleared his throat. "Mr. Collins, you have a job to do. Please escort Mr. Williams off campus as you have been ordered."

Brad stood and placed his hands on the massive, glass-covered desk and leaned toward Perry Schuster. Then, clenching his teeth, he turned away, holding out his arms toward Jake as though his wrists were manacled. "Let's go, Jake. I'll catch the bus if you can drop me off at the right entrance."

◊

The busy buzz at Mandy's dropped off almost instantly when Brad entered. Armand was in his usual chair, tilted against the wall at the back of a cluster of three tables. He was alone.

"I guess everyone else is too busy being prejudiced assholes today to make it to the Club. Pull up a chair, Brad, and join me in a discussion of the Principle of Presumed Innocence."

"Are you sure you want to be seen with a dangerous pervert, already tried, convicted, and sentenced in the court of public opinion?"

"Hell, yes! I'm a dangerous pervert, too, as anyone who lets me overhear unfounded or untrue things about you will learn the hard way." All of this was said with the resonance to ensure that no one in the shop missed a single word of it.

The Topic of Today ended up not being Presumption of Innocence or anything else remotely connected with the law. For only the second time in the history of their meetings at Mandy's, Brad and Armand talked about personal specifics, beginning with Armand righting his chair back onto four legs, leaning forward, and lowering his voice. "What are you going to do? If you need anything, I hope you have my number still in your cellphone."

eighteen

"Okay, here's the order of business with the grand jury." Jason Hartwell had assembled his team for a final briefing. "This jury has already been empaneled for six weeks, so they know the drill. There are several sharpies who can be expected to ask questions of the witnesses, but I am not anticipating any real difficulty getting our twelve votes on this one. The odds are always with us, anyway."

"I still don't know about this, Jason." Judy Taggert, a short, overweight skeptic and the youngest in the DA's office, gave him a look that declared her reservations in boldface. "The investigation has pretty much concentrated on this one suspect. You really think this is the guy? It's a lot of eggs in a loosely woven basket. You really think we can make this one stick?"

"Like dog poo on your shoe, Judy. This one is going to trial, and this guy is going to jail."

"It's all inference, circumstantial. Nothing, absolutely nothing to tie him directly to the crime, only a vague connection to the victim."

"But it's enough circumstantial evidence for me. And he's a pervert. Our perp is a perv. Proven."

"Not in any way we can use in court. If we go to all the expense of a murder one trial and blow it on appeal, what's the point?"

"When you've had as many years in the game as I have, Judy, then you'll know what I mean about the smell of conviction versus the smell of crap. I want this. I want this guy put away. Dean, grab everything. Judy, herd our witnesses. We're going to have our True Bill by this afternoon."

◊

"I have a question for the medical examiner." The young jury member with a buzz cut and a tattoo—a three-color dragon with its head peeking from below his shirt sleeve and the tail stretched above his collar—was already familiar to Jason. "Are you saying there was no biological evidence, per se, that would point to the suspect?"

Lyle McRindle, the County Coroner, answered in a practiced voice, flattened by decades of depositions and testimony. "Yes, that's what I am saying. The chemical mutilation destroyed any semen or hair fibers that might have been useful."

"What about any other, what you would call, biological clues?"

"We found some strands of hair that did not come from the victim."

"And, did you find any matches for those? Did they come from the suspect?"

"No, they did not come from the suspect."

"So, who did they come from? Did you find any matches?"

"They were matches for other members of the victim's household, which is not unexpected."

At this point Jason's discomfort was becoming evident, but there was nothing he could do, the grand jury had the absolute right to ask questions of his witnesses.

"Other members of the household? Who?" This time it was an older woman near the front of the group. Her flowered cotton dress was as plain as her face. This was the first time she had posed a question since the grand jury had convened.

"The hair strands matched samples from the stepbrother, the stepfather, and the cat." A light flutter of laughter broke the rising tension in the room.

"Can we recall the detective who interviewed the father, er, I mean stepfather, again? Yes, of course, we can. We are a grand jury." The tattooed jurist was obviously becoming rather confident in his role.

"He's already on his way back to Boston."

Mrs. Flower Dress spoke up. "Do we have to, Duane?"

At this, Jason Hartwell signaled to the court stenographer seated at the table and excused himself. The jury was now discussing the case, not asking questions of witnesses, and grand jury deliberations were required to be secret.

In the hallway, Judy edged up to him. "What happened in there?"

"The grand jury decided to recall the interviewing officer and question the stepfather and stepbrother. We are temporarily torpedoed by a damn sailor with delusions of being an admiral. This kid can be counted on to ask questions and make a few waves, but he's only one of twenty-three. He can splash around all he wants in the pool. In the end, all we need is a simple majority to indict."

Judy put on a game face for Jason and Dean, but an I-told-you-so tone was evident in her voice. "Hey, it's not over until the fat jurist sings, right?"

"Thanks for the vote of confidence, Judy. For that, you can work up a set of fresh questions for the detective and the Bellinghams and coach them on it."

◊

The requests delayed the proceedings another week, while the jury heard and returned True Bills on two other cases: a vehicular homicide from a repeat DWI offender, and a possession with intent to sell on a kid stupid enough to try to peddle cocaine to an undercover cop. The latter would probably plead out, and the former would probably go into appeal, since the accused drunk driver was a state representative.

◊

Duane, the tattooed sailor, waited impatiently for Judy to finish with her innocuous questions for the detective before plunging in. "So, officer, was Mr. Bellingham nervous when you questioned him?"

"Yes, I'd say so, but no more than anyone being questioned by a police officer?"

"What would you say his mood was, his emotions?"

"I'm a cop, not a shrink. He answered questions. He seemed worried about his daughter . . . stepdaughter. He's the one who filed the missing persons report. He was concerned."

"And the stepbrother? What was his name?"

"Jack. Jack, too. They're both named Jack."

"Okay, what about your impression of Jack number two?"

"He was, like, I don't know, a little flip. Like it was no big deal. I guess she had disappeared before. And it wasn't like she was really his kid sister. You know what I mean? Big brothers can be really protective of a younger sister."

There was a lull. Judy was wondering whether she could dismiss the detective. Then a middle-aged woman in the back waved a hand and started speaking.

"Would you say this boy loved his sister? I mean, did he seem loving toward her? When you asked him questions?"

"I don't know. I couldn't say. Again I'm not a shrink. But was he all broken up? No. Neither was the father, for that matter."

The grand jury was easier on the family, but that didn't stop them from probing in more depth about where they were and what they were doing over the weekend right after the girl had disappeared, which was the coroner's estimated time of death.

"You were on a construction job that weekend?"

Jack Bellingham scratched at his plaid flannel shirt. "Yes, I already told that to the police. I get paid better if I work on the weekend. Like overtime, but it's all just a contract. Stumpy Chase set that one up for me, I think."

"And you were gone the whole weekend? Working?"

"Yeah, except when I was sleeping in the back of Stumpy's truck. Regina wasn't back when I got home late Sunday. The next day I called Missing Persons."

◊

"And where were you, son? Do you remember?" The white-haired jury member had turned suddenly avuncular after having been aggressive on the few other occasions when he had a question.

"I was with my homies, you know. Friends. At the house, and at the Pretzky's place. All that weekend."

"Your friends would tell the same story."

"Yeah, pretty much. The ones who weren't drunk." He paused as if waiting for a laugh, but the jury hadn't found it funny.

◊

On their second day with the case, the grand jury retired to deliberate and returned a decision of No Bill. It rarely happened, since a simple majority convinced there was probable cause was all that was required to indict.

"Okay, Ms. Judy Like-I-Said, what do you think went wrong?"

"The grand jury was obviously not as convinced as you were."

"This grand jury. This grand jury expires in just over a month. The odds that the next one has an ex-submariner with a dragon tattoo and an overactive mouth are pretty slim. We'll keep digging, gather more evidence, and try again."

"Might we broaden the investigation? Maybe this guy is not our man."

"Maybe this guy is my dead uncle. Maybe this guy teaches Sunday school to orphans. I don't care. Nail him."

Dean and Judy looked at each other before either spoke. "Okay, let's dig deeper on the whole computer, database, Internet, web thing." Judy tapped rhythmically on the top of a computer monitor as she extended the list. "They say that anything you ever do is there. Forever. Nothing disappears."

Dean nodded agreement. "Okay, let's go back and see what else we can find."

nineteen

THE NEXT MONTH PASSED in a fog of anxiety for Brad as his field of vision and his life narrowed. After his teaching contract at Smith was terminated early, he was quickly dropped from the list of registered tutors on the website. With nothing on his calendar, he started filling his time with yard work for Mrs. Hathaway, raking sodden leaves from under the bushes, cleaning up debris from the recent storm, and resetting pavers that had worked their way out of position. Hanging around home put him across the street from Jenna almost every morning and afternoon, but they had switched roles; now it was Brad who pursued her.

"Here, let me help you with that." He trotted over and reached for the topmost of the cardboard boxes she was carrying.

She swiveled away from him. "I am quite capable, thank you, Bradley Williams."

"Okay, okay. Just being neighborly."

"God's forgiveness is boundless, Bradley, but I am only mortal. I still pray for you, I do, but I want nothing else to do with you. That poor girl, that poor sweet child."

"Goddamn it, Jenna. You talk as if I had already been tried and convicted."

"You don't have to curse with me, Bradley. Taking the Lord's name in—"

"I didn't do it. I. Did. Not. Do. It. Don't you understand?"

Dismayed, she licked her lips but said nothing.

He shook his head and turned to continue on his way to the corner store. Just before reaching Culligan's, a mother and her teenage daughter, part of the ubiquitous Becker clan that could be found planted over much of the county, crossed to the other side of the street as he approached.

"I'm a leper," he said. "It's right out of the movies." He stopped to pick up a bottle of ketchup at Culligan's, then continued down the street to Mandy's, the small squeeze bottle stuffed in the rear pocket of his jeans.

The Coconut Club played by their rules and did not discuss personal matters, but that did not mean that abstractions, like Justice or Exploitation or slightly more targeted generics like Statutory Rape, were off the table. Gillian had long since stopped showing up on Thursdays, but Brad kept coming around because it was the last of his outlets in a world of increasing social isolation. When the discussions finally became too uncomfortable to bear, Tom Carraway proposed that, with summer on the way, perhaps it was time for a recess.

"That won't be necessary," Brad said, pushing his chair back from the table. "I have decide to withdraw. Or quit, or whatever the term may be. I have more serious matters on my mind than arguments over semantics and syllogisms. Thank you, gentlemen. Carry on." He stood to leave, then realized he hadn't paid for his cappuccino. He slid three tens from his wallet and spread them on the table. "My treat today. Enjoy."

Were it not that the police kept coming back to question him, always with much the same questions, Brad would not have sensed the gathering storm of forces headed his way.

◊

Dean and Judy burst into Jason's office without knocking. "We found something in the transcripts from the website logs." Dean slapped a stack of paper on Jason's desk. "It didn't show up before because the girl had more than one account on InStarTute."

Judy jumped in. "We should have caught it, practically the same user name, just DeTuring2. Anyway, there's an exchange with our guy a couple days before she disappeared. Very telling."

"Do tell."

"See for yourself." She flipped open the transcript to a page with lines highlighted in bright yellow." He read aloud.

> DeTuring2: we should use the web account. safer.
> TUT0R-10: Don't worry. I miss you too much. Meet this weekend.
> DeTuring2: the usual place?
> TUT0R-10: No. Come out here.

He mumbled as he read on to himself.

"The bus to Schenectady, 'I love you, too'—it's all there." Jason did a double fist-pump and shouted, "Yes. Now we have him."

"Looks like it. With the ID from the woman at the bus station in Boston, that completes the circle."

"Great work, you two."

"We're not done. We have a forensic team combing the parking lot in Springfield. We're not hopeful. It's been months, but we could get lucky."

Jason looked up from rereading the transcript. "I think you already did. This should be enough. Let's take it to the grand jury.

twenty

"IT'S ME AGAIN."

"What's up."

"I'm under arrest. For real."

"I'll be there."

◊

"What's going to happen."

"They're going to bring you before a judge for your first appearance. Normally, this would be a well-choreographed *pas de trois*. The district attorney tries to keep you until trial or to set bail high— menace to society and all—and I push for release on own recognizance—member of community, no record, no risk of flight. Then we compromise and get you out on bond. Not likely in this case. It's murder. Rape. A minor. In the eyes of the court, you, my friend, are the veritable definition of menace to society. I don't know if I can get you out on bail."

"Which means I go to prison."

"You'll be bound over until trial, yes."

"And how long is that likely to be?"

"Months. Maybe a year. This is not a double-A game. It's the real thing, big league, and a lot is at stake."

"But I didn't do anything."

"Maybe so. Not the way they see it."

"But, I'm innocent until proven guilty. It's in the constitution, for God's sake."

"Public safety trumps that. Remember, they didn't even have to read the Boston Marathon bomber his rights."

"I'm no terrorist."

"Worse, Brad. You are a sexual predator."

"I'm not, but I'm going to jail, that's what you are saying."

"It doesn't look good, Brad, I won't lie to you."

◊

"Your Honor, the accused has no priors, not even a traffic ticket. He has lived in the community for over five years and is a lifelong resident of the Commonwealth. I submit that he is no menace to the community and is at no risk of flight. He should be released on his own recognizance."

"Your client is accused of murder and rape of a minor, violent felonies."

"My client is accused and is entering a plea of not guilty."

Hartwell looked first toward Gillian, then turned to face the magistrate. "We are asking that he be kept in custody pending trial."

Gillian persisted. "He should be released on his own recognizance."

"Recognizance is out of the question in such a case. A prudent concern for public safety would require he be held, Your Honor."

"Reasonable bail, then, Your Honor."

Hartwell persisted. "In view of the seriousness of the charges, one million cash would still be too low."

A murmur from the back of the courtroom announced the entry of Armand Richelieu, who made a beeline for Gillian. There was a quick whispered exchange, before she turned back to face the bench. "Your Honor, my client can be released into the custody of Selectman Armand Richelieu, a lifelong resident of the community, who will guarantee his appearance."

The magistrate shook his head slowly while giving the proposal some thought. "That would be most irregular, Ms. Rappaort."

"Selectman Richelieau is prepared to supervise the accused. There is precedent."

Hartwell, giving up on jail, threw back his counterproposal. "One million and the accused is under house arrest with monitoring by an electronic tracking device."

"One million is excessive, particularly in light of my client's limited financial resources. Reasonable bail would not exceed $100,000. Again, he has no priors. Again, he is a respected member of the community for whom there is no reason to regard him as at risk of flight."

"Again, I know." The magistrate shifted his gaze between the two attorneys, then to Brad. "Bail is set at $500,000. The accused is remanded into the custody of Selectman Richelieau but will be required to wear an electronic monitoring device. While out on bail, the accused will be restricted to the Richelieu residence. He is further instructed as part of the terms of his release on bail not to make use of any computer or Internet-enabled device." He banged his gavel. "Next case."

◊

In the parking lot, Brad turned his face to the cloud-shrouded sun and took in a lungful of the crisp air. "It is so good to be free."

"You are not free; you are out on bail. And you have a new piece of jewelry to show off." She tilted her head toward the bottom of his jeans where the corner of the anklet slightly puckered the material.

"Thank you for all that." Brad followed her as she weaved in and out of cars in the lot.

"It was fifteen minutes of simple haggling. The person to really thank is Armand. He's the one who bet a half million that you wouldn't catch a ride to Canada."

"I know. And I had no idea that you were so flush, Armand."

"Many things you don't know about me, my friend."

"Why did you do that?"

"Let's just say that I have good reason to believe you didn't do it."

"Good reason?"

"More than one, but we can start with the fact that it took the DA two tries to get a grand jury indictment. I think his case is weak. And"—he patted Gillian's arm—"you have a strong lawyer."

"Not yet, he doesn't. I'm just a last minute sub. He's going to need to get himself a real lawyer. I keep telling him that. Maybe he'll listen to you."

Brad patted her other arm. "I have a real lawyer: you."

"No way, Brad. Look, I was glad to help in a pinch, but this is not my bag. I do real estate, remember. You need a trial lawyer, a good one, preferably one who specializes in murder cases."

"I can't afford a good one. They had a search warrant. My laptop is now sitting in an evidence locker, and I'm not allowed even to borrow one. If I'm not working, I can't even afford the rent."

"Then the court will appoint a public defender."

"I might as well walk right back in there and confess, then."

Gillian stopped and turned to look at him with a hint of horror.

"No," he said quietly, emphatically. "No, I didn't do it, if that is what you are asking with that look. But with me, there's no such thing as innocent until proven guilty, not for this one. I'm already convicted. You've seen the local papers, the letters to the editor about sexual predators and habitual offenders who ought to be castrated before being executed. Innocent or not, I am going to jail anyway if I can't get the best defense."

"You are facing murder charges in Massachusetts. If you really do qualify for public defense, you'll get one of the best criminal lawyers available."

"I need you, Gillian. You've done this before, you were good, and you are the second or third smartest person I have ever known."

"I won't ask about the others. But no is no. You don't need me. You need a defense attorney. I worked for the other side, remember. I worked to put guys like you away." It was Brad's turn to look shocked and hurt. "No, I didn't mean it that way," she quickly continued. "I know prosecution, not defense."

It was Armand's turn to argue. "All the better. You can think like them, be two steps ahead."

"It doesn't work that way, Armand. It's a different mindset, and it takes practice and experience, experience I don't have. It's been years since I tried a case. I lost that one, too, a goddamn pusher who deliberately OD'ed a fourteen-year-old who he thought had finked on him.

"No, I just can't do it, Brad."

Brad stopped, did an about face, and headed back toward the courthouse.

"Where are you going? Did you forget something."

"Yeah, I forgot to confess."

"Don't be melodramatic. And stop acting like some self-absorbed jerk. I simply cannot do what you are asking." She took a loud breath. "I will not do what you are asking. I will not go back into that . . . that world."

"I see. I'm the one who's facing a murder charge, and you are the one who is scared." His eyes narrowed. "And you call me self-absorbed."

She opened her hand and drew it back a few inches.

"Too close to home, Counselor? You are the one who is afraid, afraid of losing."

She swallowed hard as she locked eyes with him. "Okay, I'm afraid. I'm afraid of losing a friend and being the one who failed him."

"If you don't take my case, you will have failed me. And if you take it and we lose—if we lose—I don't stop being your friend. I'll still write to you. You can visit on weekends." He grinned broadly.

"Be serious. This is the rest of your life you are talking about. Are you willing to bet that on a small-town real-estate lawyer?"

"You're relenting."

"I'm considering it."

"When do we start strategizing?"

"You are an arrogant, manipulative . . ."

"When?"

"Next Monday morning, my office. No, can't do that with you confined to quarters. I am sure Armand will not object to me coming to his place and helping to cover his bet."

"Thank you!" Brad grabbed her and kissed her square on the lips.

"None of that, now. You are my client, remember. And we have witnesses." She gave Armand a wink. "This is a professional relationship, and I have a code of ethics to follow. Plus, I have a mountain of catch-up study ahead of me, so I am going to let Armand take you to your new abode. I intend to spend today and the weekend in a law library."

twenty-one

"HARTWELL, WAIT UP." The heels on Gillian's boots echoed like a semi-automatic in the empty hallway at the courthouse in South Hadley.

"Rappaport, what a surprise it was to me to see you back. On the other side." He slowed but kept walking. "I thought you were into fence-line fights and waterfront access easements."

"Was. How did you get this plum, Jason?"

"Stuck in my thumb."

"Still quick witted, I see. You know, I am going to turn your plum into a stewed prune."

"And the lady lawyer has the wits to match. But I don't think you have the chops for this case."

"You don't think so? What do you have?"

Hartwell stopped and turned with military crispness. "Everything. We can tie your client to the victim and the crime. We have phone records, computer records, and chemical evidence, plus physical evidence at the scene. This case is a piece of cake."

"Tut-tut. You're mixing metaphors. Plum pudding, perhaps."

"So? This time your guy is going down."

"What do you mean this time?"

"He has a record, his own daughter."

"The charges were dropped. You can't use that. It won't be allowed in evidence."

"That depends on many things, as well you know. Once I get your guy on the stand . . ."

"He doesn't have to testify."

"Oh, you have been away from the game way too long, Rappaport. Your guy doesn't take the stand, and it's as good as a confession. That may not be the law, but in this kind of case, that is precisely how the jury will see it, judge's instructions before deliberation notwithstanding. Case closed. Cell door closed. One less pervert walks the street."

"Do you cook, Jason?"

"What?"

"Ever try making plum pudding? It's tricky. If you're not careful it falls flat." She started to walk away. "I'll see you in court for pretrial. I look forward to seeing what you have. And when we go to trial, I expect to boil you in your own pudding and bury you and your career with a stick of holly in your heart."

"Very literary. Certainly you are not threatening an officer of the court."

"No, only making a prediction about the outcome of this case. Be careful what and how you cook."

"Oh, we will, Counselor. We would not want to help establish grounds for appeal. Wait until you see the evidence. If there's anything exculpatory in there, I'll eat it. Smothered in butter-rum sauce."

Gillian smiled. "Nice to see you again, Hartwell. I mean that."

Hartwell let his own smile broaden. "And it's good to see you again, Gillian. And I mean that as well."

◊

Gillian put her boots up on the desk, then immediately took them down. "I keep forgetting, this is Armand's home office, not mine."

"What made you change your mind and accept my case?"

"Hartwell clinched it with his bravado. I think he has allowed himself to move this case along too fast. Knowing Jason, it was probably over the advice of at least one of his team, and I even have a guess who it would be." She twirled one errant strand of hair. "We'll have to wait to get what he has in discovery. I am still wrestling with whether or not to put you on the stand."

"No, I won't testify. I told you that."

"What the DA told me was right. The jury will conclude you have something to hide if you don't defend yourself."

"Or that I don't need to defend myself."

"So, now you're the legal expert. How am I going to sell that to a jury?"

"I don't know, but that's your job, isn't it?"

She leaned forward, hands folded on the desktop. "But you have to give me the tools I need to do my job."

"I'll give you everything I can, but I won't take the stand."

"Why? What do you have to hide?"

"So now you are the jury. I told you, I didn't do it. How many times do I have to say it before you believe me?"

"Then why won't you testify?"

"I thought it was my constitutional right. I didn't do it; I didn't kill her."

"Okay, okay," she said, holding up a hand in protest. "You don't need to keep saying that. I took your case already. We are going to trial. I'll plan my case without your testimony."

"Good of you, Gillian. But sometimes it doesn't seem as if you believe I'm innocent."

"What I believe doesn't matter; what the jury believes is what counts."

He locked eyes with her. "It matters to me, that you believe and trust me."

"It shouldn't. Frankly, as your lawyer, strictly your lawyer, I don't care if you did do it. As I said, I don't even want you to tell me if you did—that would make giving you the best defense more challenging—but it's no longer about you or about guilt or innocence. It's about conduct in a court of law. It's a system of rules, a game, like chess, like the rules that guide your work in mathematics."

"Not at all the same. Mathematics is about the pursuit of truth, about proof."

"The same as the law, at least that's the story they told us in law school. I think I believed that story. Mostly. The methods of proof may be different, the pursuit a different process, but it's pretty much the same game."

"The stakes are higher."

"Yes, that. In some cases. In this case. Which is why you need to stop worrying about whether I trust you or believe in you. Worry about whether you trust me, whether you believe in me, because, with you not taking the stand, your life is literally in my hands."

◊

"Well, turns out the DA's case is pretty much as we expected except for this." She slid the stapled sheath of papers toward Brad with her index finger.

"What is it?"

"You tell me."

Brad started reading the transcript of the online session. "But this is impossible. This didn't happen. I never . . ." He kept reading in silence.

"It's pretty damning, Brad. I don't know what to make of it or how to deal with it."

"It's the wrong . . . it's not her. DeTuring, that was her handle. This is DeTuring2."

"It's her, they verified it. Just another account. And there she is, agreeing to meet you just before she was killed."

"It's a frame-up. Faked. Something."

"That doesn't make sense, Brad. Who would frame you and why? This is show-stopping evidence. It may not put you at the scene of the crime, but it shows opportunity and premeditation."

"Something is wrong here, and we just have to look carefully enough to find it."

"Our only hope is your alibi. I told them about your antics."

"You tipped your hand? You told them what your defense is going to be?"

"I have to in a case like this. If the defendant has an alibi, you have to present this to the judge, and he rules on whether going to trial is worth the expense to the Commonwealth. A murder trial is doubly costly, because if you are . . . if you were convicted, there's a mandatory appeal in this state.

"Look, this is just part of a complicated pretrial process. A lot of things could change. I have motions to file, including a Motion to Dismiss based on the lack of direct evidence. I might have a more credible case on the alibi if you could just remember the name of your girlfriend."

"Not my girlfriend. We just . . . we had a fling. We were two lonely teachers on the loose in New Haven."

"Yeah, right. And Judge Musselman did not accept that alibi, citing two reasons. First is the uncertainty of the time of death. It's a two or three-day window because of the delay in finding the body. Second, you can account for most of that time span, but you have no proof or corroboration for the critical last part of it."

"I told you, I was with this woman."

"This woman whose name you don't even remember."

"I remember her name: Trini. I just don't remember her last name. I told you, she was a teacher, from somewhere in Massachusetts, or maybe New York, but I don't think she ever told me the town. Check the conference registrations."

"We have already checked the list. There were no Trinis, no Trinas. Both Katrinas checked out and have no memory of meeting you, much less having an affair with you. The one Catrina is in her seventies—definitely not the woman you described."

"Then we have to check them all, all the women. She was, like in her late twenties, early thirties, about so high, pretty, brown hair—"

"We've been through this, Brad. There were some 300 teachers from five states registered for the conference. Two-thirds of them were women. They didn't fill out forms with height and age or preference in men. If only you had cared enough to bother to get her name. I don't understand men. How can you have slept with someone and not know her name? How?"

"I don't know about men, Gillian. But for me, that's not what we talked about, that wasn't what it was about."

She put her face in her hands. "No, it sure wasn't."

"Fuck you, Gillian. I live the life of a damn monk most of the time. I just closed down that part of myself when I moved out here."

"Except when you were cyber-stalking teenagers."

Brad drew circles on the yellow pad in front of him, breaking the lead on his pencil, then tearing through the top sheet. He threw the pencil at the table, sending it bouncing onto a bookshelf.

"I'm sorry, Brad."

"I didn't do it. I told you exactly the extent of my so-called cyber-stalking."

"I know. Let's go back to what the DA has and how we're going to deal with it without you taking the stand. We'll keep trying to find this Trini."

twenty-two

GILLIAN REACHED HIM by phone at Armand's. The week before, his house arrest had been reinforced by the lease on his apartment being terminated for non-payment of rent. Armand had recovered what few things of value remained at Mrs. Hathaway's.

"You, okay?"

"Yeah, just trying to get used to being chauffeured to and from the courthouse in a patrol car."

"Well, we are one step closer, now that *voir dire* is complete. I think jury selection went pretty well, don't you?"

"I'll take your word for it. I didn't follow everything. I think I was distracted."

"Really? Well, the bottom line is that we got a fairly educated group, which should help. We have those two businessmen, the engineer and the dentist, one college professor, that housewife who blogs and writes short stories, and the former third-grade teacher. Plus a mechanic and a retired merchant marine. Who knows about them. Oh yes, and that 25-year-old who lives at home and plays video games. Who knows."

"I thought we didn't want any school teachers."

"You're right, we didn't want teachers. Or social workers or anyone who works with kids, anyone who is more likely to be too sympathetic to the prosecutor's case. But I had no cause and had already used up all my peremptory challenges. This is what we got, and I think we will be okay.

"Gender balance is good, too: seven men and five women with one each in the alternates. In cases like this, men may be less likely to convict than women. In your case we would have to qualify that to men without teenage daughters. Anyone with a daughter is a problem, of course, but we could hardly eliminate every potential juror with a daughter."

"You're the lawyer. I'll assume you know what you are talking about. Right now I just want to get this behind me and go home, if home is still an option. Four days. Four days of legal limbo, then . . ."

"That's how long the trial itself is expected to last; how long the jury might take in deliberation is impossible to guess."

"Is it true that the longer they deliberate, the more it's likely to favor the defense?"

"That's the urban legend, anyway. If it's valid, hope for a long and anxious wait."

"I meant to ask, what ever happened to your big pretrial motion?"

"The Motion to Dismiss? The judge deferred his ruling until after the prosecution presents its case. If he then agrees that the evidence is patently inadequate, he can issue a directed verdict of not guilty."

"And?"

"We will have to see exactly what the prosecution presents and how. Hartwell has three key witnesses: an engineer from an independent data recovery lab, a technician from the web-hosting service that operated the tutoring site, and the county coroner."

"And we have?"

"We have you, but you won't testify. And we have me. Plus, we do have the witnesses we need."

"Not that I fully approve."

"We discussed it and discussed it. You have to trust me on all this."

◊

The opening argument from the prosecution was hardly the stuff of television legal drama. Jason Hartwell, in the short, controlled sentences of his courtroom persona, outlined what the prosecution would prove. He never missed an opportunity to remind the jury of the heinous nature of the crime and the age of the victim.

Brad listened but remained detached, ever the observer watching for patterns. The story of the rest of his life was being written before his eyes, and he was occupied with sentence structure and counting words. This obsession was, as it always had been for him, the ultimate defense of a spinning mind arming itself against the assault of reality.

Gillian used a tactic that was new to Brad, deferring her opening statement until after the prosecution finished its case. This, she explained, effectively gave her virtual back-to-back summations and enabled her to tailor her opening gambit to the already completed prosecution arguments. "I trust you," was all he said when she asked what he thought of it.

Hartwell, whose ambition and love for the dramatic remained hidden behind his simple grammar, began his case by calling Lyle McRindle, County Coroner, to the stand.

"Your Honor, Defense has stipulated to the witness's qualifications as an expert." Gillian sat back down and scribbled a quick note to Brad: "McRindel's their big hitter. Should save him as a closer."

The County Coroner was a calm pro on the stand, and Hartwell, with his methodical manner, worked him effectively.

"From your autopsy, Dr. McRindel, were you able to determine the cause of death?"

"I was."

"And what was your conclusion."

"Blunt trauma to the skull. The victim was struck on the forehead with a heavy, irregular object, probably a rock. There were rock fragments in the wound. She was repeatedly bludgeoned from behind with the same or a similar object, also evidenced by mineral fragments in the tissue.

"The victim's body was naked from the waist down when found, with only an open blouse on top. We were unable to find the rest of her clothes in the area. From abrasions on her knees and left arm, it appears that she had tried to run from her assailant and fell on rough ground. It is possible that the blow to her forehead occurred when it struck a rock as she fell."

"What else did you find?"

"The victim's body had been mutilated, chemically burned with a caustic agent."

Hartwell retrieved a set of large, mounted photographs from his table and approached the witness stand again. "I have here prosecution exhibits 1 through 6. Do you recognize these photos, Dr. McRindel?"

"Yes, I do."

"Can you tell the court what they are?"

"Yes, they are enlargements of the photographs taken during the autopsy I performed on the victim. My initials can be seen at the bottom right."

"Thank you, Dr. McRindel."

"Objection." Gillian had risen slowly, as if uncertain how to proceed.

Judge Musselman narrowed his eyes. "On what grounds, Counselor?"

"May we approach the bench, Your Honor?"

The judge waved them up and leaned forward as they approached. In a lowered voice he said, "Now tell me what this is about. You knew the coroner's report would be entered into evidence at pre-trial; that was the time to raise any objections."

"This is not the coroner's report, Your Honor. These are full-color, 17-by-22 glossy enlargements of close-up views of the nude victim's mutilated body. This is blatant sensationalism on the part of the prosecution. The provocative and disturbing nature of these photos can only serve to inflame the jury. Defense has already stipulated acceptance of Dr. McRindel as an expert. His testimony as an expert is sufficient."

Hartwell spoke through clenched teeth. "The photographs go to the heinous nature of the crime."

"The heinous nature of the crime is not at issue, Your Honor. The guilt or innocence of the defendant is. The photographs are irrelevant to establishing that guilt or innocence."

"Are you lecturing me on basic jurisprudence, Counselor?"

"Not at all, Your Honor."

"Then perhaps you can tell me how we can know what relevance the photographs have before the prosecution has made his case with them?"

"Have you seen them, Your Honor?"

Musselman was clearly not expecting that. His mouth turned down. "Ms. Rappaport, Mr. Hartwell, you may step back." He raised his voice to address the courtroom. "Court is in recess for fifteen minutes." He banged his gavel with extra force, picked up the photos, and left for his chambers.

"What was that all about?" Brad asked when Gillian returned to the table.

"If you had seen the photos, you would understand. I don't want the jury to see them."

"Why? Are they that bad?"

"Worse. I hope you had a light lunch. With or without the pictures, the coroner's testimony won't be easy to take."

◊

With the exception of the jury, most of the people in the room were chatting when the judge reentered and the bailiff called, "All rise!"

"I have decided to allow the photos to be entered into evidence. The jury is warned that they are graphic and could be upsetting. The prosecution may proceed with the witness."

Hartwell stacked the photos on an easel in view of McRindel, Judge Musselman, and the jury. The front-most shot, from an overhead camera, showed the girl's body from roughly mid-thigh to just below the navel. The middle third of the image was a grisly pudding of unrecognizable tissue and exposed bone. Her arms were crossed at the wrist, but the hands had been mostly eaten away. The jury gasped almost in unison, and Brad closed his eyes.

"Please tell us in your own words, Dr. McRindel, the results of your examination and your conclusions from it."

"The body was mutilated after death. From the pattern of chemical burns and decomposition, it is possible to establish that the chemical was first introduced into the interior of the body through the vagina, possibly with a funnel or tubing of some kind, then a substantial quantity was splashed liberally over the entire pelvic region. Her arms had first been positioned so the hands, too, would be mutilated. The result is that there was no chance to recover hair or tissue samples under the fingernails."

"Could you identify the chemical used."

"Yes, it was a mixture of potassium hydroxide and sodium hydroxide, commonly found in drain cleaner."

"Were you able to determine the kind of drain cleaner used on the body?"

"Yes. Many of the major brands have additives—odorants, coloring agents, and such—that enable identification. This had none of those, so the lab report concludes it was a generic formula, such as is commonly sold in bulk."

"And what was the effect of this chemical on the body."

"As you can see from this picture and the close-ups, the effect, known as alkaline hydrolysis, was to partially dissolve the tissue." Hartwell removed the first picture from the easel and slowly exposed successive shots. Quiet groans and vocal exhalations could be heard around the room.

"Why would anyone do this?"

"Objection."

"Sustained."

"What were the consequences of the use of this chemical on this part of the body?"

"The tissue has been denatured and largely destroyed. It was not possible to recover semen or other usable DNA from this area."

"And did you reach any conclusion with respect to these findings?"

"Yes, I concluded that she had probably been sexually assaulted."

"Thank you. No further questions."

Gillian approached the witness for the cross-examination. "So, Dr. McRindel, let me understand. You conclude that the victim was sexually assaulted because there is no evidence of sexual assault. Is that correct?"

"No. In as much as the chemical appeared to have first been introduced vaginally, an attempt to cover up any evidence from a sexual assault is a reasonable conclusion."

"Is it consistent with any other conclusion, Doctor?"

"Well, yes, of course. The killer could be a psychopath with a hatred for female genitalia or—"

Hartwell objected. "Defense is asking the witness to speculate outside his area of expertise."

"Sustained."

"Within your expertise, Doctor, is it possible that the use of chemicals was not an attempt to cover up evidence of sexual assault?"

"Yes, but—"

"Thank you. Now, you stated in your report that you judged the victim had been dead approximately nine days. Can you be more precise?"

"Yes, she was killed sometime within a forty-eight-hour window starting at noon on Friday, the first of March."

"I am impressed with that precision. How is it that you can be so exact about a body that was not recovered for over a week?"

"Because in this case we had detailed information about the temperature and other conditions of the shallow grave in which she was buried—it was just above freezing—and we have two independent countdown clocks as it were: the chemical reaction of the caustics with the tissue and the biological decomposition of the unaffected tissue. Aside from the alkaline hydrolysis of the pelvic region, the body was quite well preserved by the cold conditions."

"So you are saying she could not possibly have been killed before noon on Friday or after noon on Sunday?

"No, I am saying that the most probable time of death falls within that window."

"And you're certain about those times?"

"Yes, actually those times include a generous margin of error. My report fixes the time of death at two o'clock, Saturday morning, plus or minus six hours."

"Would you stake your reputation on those times?"

"Objection."

"Sustained."

"Dr. McRindel, how certain are you about the time of death?"

"I am confident in the estimated time of death; I would stake my reputation on the time of death being within that forty-eight-hour window."

At the prosecution table, Hartwell removed his hand from over his eyes. "Redirect, Your Honor."

"Proceed."

"Dr. McRindel, would you say forensic medicine is an exact science?"

"No, of course not."

"Is it possible, is there any possibility, however remote, that the time of death was outside what you referred to as that forty-eight-hour window?"

"Well, yes, remotely possible, but—"

"Thank you. That will be all."

◊

With the dramatic opening behind him, Hartwell moved on to systematically establishing the connection to Bradley Williams. First came testimony on evidence retrieved from Brad's apartment, which included a blue plastic rollerball pen, the identical twin of one found a few feet from the body.

On cross examination, Gillian gestured with a pen as she talked. "Some prints were recovered from the pen. Is that correct?"

"Yes."

"And could you find matches for any of those prints?"

"They were partials, one a partial thumbprint that was not sufficient for a certain match but might have been from the accused."

"Is that the same as saying it might have been from someone else?"

"It did not rule out the accused."

"Please answer the question. Could the partial print have been from someone else?"

"Yes."

Gillian casually set her pen on the witness stand as she crossed in front. "The pen you found and dusted for prints, was it like mine?"

"Objection. Defense Counsel's pen has not been introduced into evidence."

Judge Musselman leaned forward. "Are you going somewhere with these theatrics, Counselor?"

"I withdraw the question." She turned away. "The rollerball found at the scene of the crime and the one obtained when the defendant's apartment was searched, how were they the same?"

"They are the same model from the same manufacturer."

"Millions of rollerballs and ball point pens from the same manufacturer will look alike. Is there anything unique or distinctive about these two pens?

"Yes, they both bear the same custom imprints."

"What are those imprints?"

"The logos of WesLee Web Hosting and of the InStarTute math tutoring website."

"So, these are promotional pens, the sort that are given away for advertising, am I correct?"

"They appear to be."

"Thank you. No further questions."

As she turned away, the witness picked up the pen in front of him and held it out toward her. "Don't forget your pen."

"Oh, that's all right. I have a couple more just like it." She pulled several identical rollerball pens from her jacket pocket.

A crime lab technician was the next witness for the prosecution. A pair of rubber gloves and a near-empty plastic bottle of drain cleaner, obtained from Brad's apartment, were introduced into evidence. The technician testified that the remaining contents of the bottle were consistent with the effects on the body and with the chemical residue retrieved from the crime scene.

Holding the lab report in her hand, Gillian approached the woman for cross examination. "Regarding this report on the chemical used, is it possible to determine where the chemical used on the body, the drain cleaner, was obtained?"

"The profile of the chemical residue from the body was consistent with formulae used in generic store brands and drain cleaner sold in bulk. This matched the ingredients of the generic drain cleaner in the bottle obtained from the defendant's apartment."

"So, you would be unable to tell whether the chemical used on the victim's body came from, say, Market Basket or Shaw's or a local plumbing supply store, correct?"

"Yes. It would not be possible."

"And this particular bottle, Prosecution Exhibit 7, from the accused's apartment, could you ascertain where it was purchased?"

"Yes, it bears a price sticker from Meecham's Hardware, a local chain with several stores in the area, including West Hopeland."

"Could you read for the court the warning on the bottle, the first line of the second paragraph?"

"Yes, of course. It says, 'Caution: Always wear protective rubber gloves when using this product.'"

"So, one would expect to find rubber gloves along with this product?"

"Objection."

"I'll rephrase the question. In view of the warning label, it would not be unusual for a pair of rubber gloves to be found in proximity to such a product, would it?"

"No, it would not be unusual."

Next to testify was a digital forensics technician from a data recovery service used by the Commonwealth to analyze the content of computer hard drives in criminal cases. He testified to finding several items linking the accused to the victim, including an annotated PDF copy of a mathematics paper with the same file name as a similar file found on Regina Bellingham's computer. Timestamps on the files and comments within the paper traced back as far as early January. There was also a PDF printout of a newspaper article with a picture of Regina Bellingham on Brad's computer. His browser history and cookies indicated regular visits to InStarTute.com throughout the months leading up to the death of the victim.

On cross examination, Gillian started aggressively. "Did you find any evidence of criminal activity on the computer hard-drive?"

"No."

"Did you find any pornography on the hard-drive?"

"No."

"Did you find any evidence of tampering, erasures, or other attempts to destroy or hide information?"

"No, only the usual deleted files, including previous versions of the victim's writings."

"From your analysis, was there any evidence that would suggest that the defendant had anything to hide or had attempted to hide anything?"

"Objection. Asking for a conclusion."

"Withdrawn."

A telephone company representative was called and a phone log was entered into evidence recording a single telephone call to Brad's cell phone from a cellphone registered to the victim.

Gillian told Brad that the evidence was all small potatoes and completely circumstantial, but she knew full well that the picture being painted was of a patient predator stalking his victim.

twenty-three

THE SECOND DAY of the trial began with the prosecution calling Malcolm Muybridge Todd.

A skinny, somewhat nervous young man with his hair gelled and spiked took the stand and was sworn in.

"Are you employed, Mr. Todd?"

"Yes, sir, at WesLee Hosting."

"And just what business is WesLee Hosting in?"

"They operate a computer server farm that hosts websites."

"And what is your job at this company."

"I'm Lead Software Engineer."

"Could you explain to the court what that job means, what your duties are?"

"I oversee maintenance programming. I write and test code for computers. I'm responsible for keeping the servers up-to-date and running correctly. I also take care of the backend programming for certain sites."

"Could you explain what you mean by 'backend programming'?"

"That's the code that actually makes that particular site work the way it does."

"Do you recognize this document, previously marked Prosecution

Exhibit 9? Is that your signature on the first page?"

"Yes, I do. That's my signature."

"Now, could you tell the court what this document is and how it came to bear your signature."

"This is a dump, a printout, of the user activity log for the InStarTute site, a site we host and manage at WesLee. I signed it when the police asked me to. This is the part covering the week of 24 February of this year."

"I direct your attention to the top of page 23. Could you tell the court what is the date and time indicated on this particular portion of the log?"

"It's from Wednesday, 27 February, 6:27:32pm.

"Would you read for us what begins at the third line down from the top?"

Malcolm began to read aloud from the transcript:

DeTuring2: i saw your flag. i thought u were at some conference
TUT0R-10: Came back early. We need to meet.

"That's enough for the moment. Can you tell the court the meaning of these terms, 'detouring-two' and 'tutor-ten'? What do they refer to?"

"Those are online handles, user names for account holders. Users do not use their real names. Security and privacy policy, you know. All messages are identified only by online handles."

"Is it possible to obtain the real identity of users from their handles?"

"Yes, but only by someone within WesLee with the proper administrative clearance. Or a school official. Oh, yes, the police, law enforcement, you know, with a warrant. Like in this case."

"Can you tell the court the full real identity of these two people here referred to as detouring-two and tutor-ten?"

"Yes. According to our records, DeTuring2 is a student, a senior at Ipswich High School, Regina Elizabeth Josephson Bellingham. TUTOR-10 is one of the registered math tutors for that site, Mr. Bradley James Williams of West Hopeland."

"Thank you. Would you please continue to read from the transcript, just to the bottom of the page."

Malcolm read:

> DeTuring2: we should use the web account. safer.
> TUTOR-10: Don't worry. I miss you too much. Meet this weekend.
> DeTuring2: the usual place?
> TUTOR-10: No. Come out here.
> DeTuring2: how? u know i don't have a car.
> TUTOR-10: OK. Take the bus.
> DeTuring2: which?
> TUTOR-10: Give me a minute.
> DeTuring2: kk

"Let me interrupt here. Can you tell us what this 'kay-kay' means?"

"It's online shorthand for okay, okay."

"Shorthand. I see." There was a ripple of suppressed laughter. "Please continue."

> TUTOR-10: Take the late bus to Schenectady but get off at Springfield. Friday. I'll pick you up in the parking lot at Main and Congress. Be careful.
> DeTuring2: i will. can't wait to be with you
> TUTOR-10: I'll see you Friday nite.
> DeTuring2: i luv u.
> TUTOR-10: Ya, me too.

"The session ended there and both parties logged out."

"Thank you, Mr. Todd. That will be all."

Gillian took her time, flipping back through her notes before approaching the witness stand. "Tell me, Mr. Todd, is there any way those records could have been falsified or altered in some way?"

"Objection. Asking the witness to speculate."

"Your Honor, Mr. Todd is testifying as a credentialed professional with expert knowledge of the technical operations of his employer."

"Objection overruled."

"I'll repeat the question. Is there any way those records could have been falsified or altered in some way?"

"No."

"No way at all? How is that?"

"Because we have ways to tell if files have been tampered with, checksums. And the log files are encrypted."

"Encrypted. What does that mean?"

"They're encoded, a code. You have to know the key, like a password, in order to even open them."

"And who knows this key, this password?"

"My boss, Mr. Herald, the Operations Manager, also the COO, Chief Operating Officer."

Gillian picked up the log. "But it's your signature on this document indicating that you opened the file and printed it out. Is that correct? Did you have the Operations Manager or the COO enter the key for you?"

"No. I have the key, too. I need it to be able to work on the files."

"What sort of work would that be? What would you need to do with the files?"

"Uh, like manually correct errors or fix some other transaction."

"Alter the files?"

"Objection. The witness is not on trial."

"Your Honor, my question goes to the integrity of the evidence. But I will rephrase. Mr. Todd, is it possible for you or anyone with the appropriate access to the files to make changes to them."

"Well, yes. But—"

"Thank you. Can you tell me, Mr. Todd, has anyone ever, to your knowledge, gained improper or illegal access to the websites operated by WesLee Hosting?"

"Not really, we have firewalls, systems that prevent that."

"Please correct me if I am wrong, but aren't computers frequently broken into by so-called hackers."

"Well, yes. It happens."

"How often? How often would you say? How often at WesLee Hosting, particularly the InStarTute site?"

"Not that often?"

"Not that often? What about over 200 times a week?"

"Objection. Putting words in the witness's mouth."

"Is it part of your job to keep track of attempts to break into the computers at WesLee."

"Yes."

"And do you recall how many such attempts occurred last week for the InStarTute site?"

"Yes."

"How many attempted break-ins were there, Mr. Todd?"

"Most of those were just port scans that—"

"Just answer the question. How many?"

"Over 200. We have a lot of users at the colleges and universities who—"

"Thank you. Do any of those attempts ever succeed? Do they ever manage to open or alter files in your computers?"

"Not really."

"Do you recall an incident last year when websites hosted by WesLee were hacked, broken into, and student information was illegally downloaded?"

"Yes, but that was—"

"Thank you Mr. Todd. By any chance would you have one of these blue logo rollerballs, like this?"

"Yes, of—"

"Objection."

"Withdrawn, Your Honor. No further questions."

◊

During the noon recess, Gillian confronted Brad. "I still don't know what to believe about the log transcript. My stab at its credibility was an act of desperation, and I don't expect the jury to buy it. People put their trust in computer records, telephone logs, online data. Whether justified or not, they assume that the records are accurate."

"I told, you, I did not have that online conversation. I don't know what to believe either. It didn't happen."

"Then what did? That computer file didn't just create itself."

"I'm stumped. That kid—don't you find him a bit odd?"

"He's a computer geek. They're all a bit odd."

"I was thinking as you were cross-examining him that there was something, something almost familiar about him, but I can't put my finger on it."

"Well, right now we have to move on. Hartwell is calling his last witness, your friend, Dr. Sousa."

"I thought you said he couldn't."

"I did, but during pre-trial, the judge said he'd allow it. I'll object again for the record, in hopes that it might be useful on appeal, but I'll be overruled again. She is going to testify, and I don't think she is going to be a very good character witness on your behalf."

"You can make her look bad."

"Which could backfire. Let me see exactly what Hartwell has and where he is going. Then I'll try to tack upwind, take the wind from his sails."

"I didn't know you were a sailor."

"Not, but I'm great with maritime metaphors." She smiled and put her hand on his back. "Okay, back into the maelstrom."

◊

Hartwell called Dr. Susan Charlotte Sousa to the stand, Gillian objected, and Judge Musselman overruled her.

After preliminary questions about her qualifications and experience, Hartwell got to the point. "You had the defendant in therapy for two years, is that correct, Dr. Sousa?"

"I had the defendant and his daughter in therapy together for just under two years."

"And his daughter? Isn't that unusual?"

"Objection."

"Sustained."

Hartwell took a step back. "Could you tell the court why you were seeing the defendant along with his daughter in therapy?"

"Objection."

"Overruled. Please answer the question."

"Mr. Williams had been accused of molesting his daughter."

"Move to strike."

Judge Musselman tilted his head down to look over the tops of his glasses. "Counselor, you will have your turn. Overruled."

Hartwell suppressed a smile. "Based on your expertise, Dr. Sousa, and from your experience in treating the defendant—the defendant and his daughter—what can you tell us about the defendant?"

"Objection."

"Overruled." The judge was clearly becoming annoyed. "Counselor, you are pushing it here. Prosecution may proceed."

"Dr. Sousa?"

Thrown off by the legal ping-pong, Dr. Sousa frowned in confusion. "Could you repeat the question?"

"Please share your conclusions about the defendant, based on your expert knowledge and your work with him . . . and his daughter."

"Bradley Williams is an intelligent, socially immature, loner. He has difficulty understanding appropriate limits and recognizing boundaries."

"Could you explain what you mean by that, Doctor?"

"He sometimes fails to acknowledge the legitimacy of limits on behavior. He does not always seem to know when behaviors are appropriate and when they are not."

"Like sexual behaviors?"

"Objection. Leading the witness."

"Sustained." The judge let out a sigh of reluctance.

"Can you be more specific, with examples, Doctor?"

"He had difficulty understanding how behaviors, such as hugging, can be appropriate in some circumstances and not others. He had particular difficulty understanding the role of age and power in relationships, especially when it comes to sexuality."

"Again, could you explain what you mean by 'the role of age and power in relationships, especially when it comes to sexuality'?"

"At the time of the abuse, his daughter was nine years—"

"Move to strike."

"Granted. The jury will disregard the last statement. Prosecution may proceed."

"We have no further questions, your honor."

"Defense?"

"Just a few questions, Doctor. Were the defendant and his daughter in therapy with you because of any court order?"

"No. They came of their own accord."

"Do you recall why they came to you?"

"Yes, they wanted to work on their relationship after the divorce between Mr. Williams and his then wife."

"Was there a problem with the relationship? Had something happened?"

"Yes, his daughter had accused him of sexually molesting her, then changed her story."

"What do you mean, 'changed her story'?"

"She claimed she had lied. She—"

"Objection. Hearsay."

"I'll withdraw the question. No further questions."

Hartwell stood. "Redirect, Your Honor. Can you tell me, Dr. Sousa, whether children ever change their story to please their parents?"

"Objection. Irrelevant."

"Sustained."

"Withdrawn. The Prosecution rests."

"Court stands in recess until ten o'clock tomorrow morning." The judge banged his gavel.

twenty-four

WITH THE JUDGE'S RULING on the Motion to Dismiss that the trial would proceed, the third day began with Gillian's opening statement followed by the moment that Brad had dreaded.

"Defense calls Angela Beatrice Williams to the stand."

Brad started to stand, turning to face Gillian.

"Mr. Williams,"—a bang of the gavel—"sit down!"

Brad glared at Gillian and spoke quietly between clenched teeth. "Do you have to?"

"Mr. Williams." The judge spoke with a rising inflection. "Sit down or I shall have to hold you in contempt of court."

Gillian placed a hand on Brad's shoulder and firmly guided him back into the chair. "Your Honor, if it please the court, I'd like a word with my client."

"Are you calling the witness or not?"

"Yes, but just a word."

Gillian put her forehead against Brad's and spoke in a tone so low that Brad could barely hear. "You won't testify; somebody has to do it for you."

"Not my daughter. It's not her fight."

"It is. She doesn't want to have to be reduced to exchanging letters with a prisoner. You're still her father. She is not nine-years-old anymore, and she wants to do this."

Brad closed his eyes and lowered his head almost to the yellow legal pad on the table in front of him. "Okay," he said, his voice full of defeat. "Okay."

◊

Brad had to admit, his daughter was poised on the stand, handling the preliminary questions with quiet firmness and without hesitation.

"So, you lied to the judge, in the custody hearing?"

"Yes, I told him what I thought my mother wanted me to say. I didn't really understand what was going on."

"What changed your mind?"

"A social worker told me about jail and what they, quote-unquote, do to bad men who do bad things with little girls. I knew I had lied. But somehow I thought it only meant I could stay with my mother. I didn't understand it meant I couldn't see my dad. I told the social worker that he hadn't done anything. She wouldn't believe me."

"What did you do when she didn't believe you?"

"I waited until my mother was out shopping, and I called my father's attorney. By this time, he, my father, was charged with indecent assault on a minor. It took months to get another custody hearing and then . . . well, eventually the charges were dropped, but Dad couldn't live in Sudbury anymore."

"Thank you, Angela." She sent a grim smile toward Brad, then turned to Hartwell. "Your witness."

Hartwell approached the stand and leaned on the railing. "Tell me, Angela, do you know what perjury is?"

"Objection. The prosecution is asking the witness to interpret the law."

"Your honor, it goes to credibility."

"I'll allow it.

"Let me rephrase the question. Do you understand the penalties for perjury?"

"I do."

"Do you understand that contradicting yourself under oath constitutes perjury?"

"I understand. I lied then. I perjured myself. I am not lying now."

"And how can we know that?"

"Objection."

"Withdrawn."

Gillian rose to her feet. "Redirect, Your Honor."

"Proceed."

"How old were you when you lied in the custody hearing?"

"Nine. I had just turned nine."

"Thank you, Angela. No further questions, Your Honor. Defense calls Virgil Danforth Sandborg."

Virgil Sandborg, a balloon of a man in a sports jacket that could not be buttoned, waddled his way to the stand and was sworn in.

"You were at a conference for science teachers with the accused earlier this year, is that correct?"

"Yes. Science and math. And tech. Yes."

"Can you tell me how you got to that conference?"

"Brad picked me up at my place just before four p.m. on Wednesday. That would be the twenty-seventh. He had a borrowed car."

"That was February of this year, right?"

"Yes. We drove down to New Haven that afternoon because the conference, NEW-STEM, started early in the morning, and I didn't want to miss the first session."

"How long did it take to drive from West Hopeland down to New Haven?"

"Well, we took I-91, of course, but we ran into heavy traffic around Hartford and again into New Haven. Then Brad couldn't find the hotel where the conference was being held. He's a math teacher, but he refuses to use a GPS, would you believe. It took us over two-and-a-half hours before we checked in at the hotel."

"So, let me see if this is correct. From just before four o'clock on Wednesday afternoon until sometime after 6:30 that night, you were in a car with the defendant, riding to New Haven."

"Yes, that's right. In fact, I remember the clock in my room when I checked in. It was nearly seven."

"Tell me, did the defendant have a computer with him?"

"Yes, he brought his laptop. We all did. Hey, we're geeks." He smiled broadly.

"And did either of you use your laptops while driving to New Haven?"

"No, they were in the trunk. It was a small car. And what would we do with them on the highway, anyway? It's not like we had Wi-Fi and could surf the Web or anything."

"So, the defendant was with you the entire time from 4 to roughly 6:30 on Wednesday, the 27th of February, and at no point during that time did he make use of his laptop. Is that correct?"

Hartwell sighed. "Asked and answered."

"I just wanted to verify the precise time and circumstances of the trip to New Haven. And after you got there, were you also with Mr. Williams?"

"No, only for dinner on Wednesday night. He's math, I'm biology, and we were always in different sessions. I did see Brad, Mr. Williams, several times with some teacher, a woman that he met at the conference. Looked like they were old friends or something, very intensely into each other."

"Did you know this other teacher? Had you seen her before."

"No, but I remember she was short and kinda cute, long brown hair."

Hartwell began his cross examination by asking about the time of arrival in New Haven.

"Yes, it was about 6:30 at night."

"Did you check your watch when you last saw the defendant?"

"No, but I remember the clock in my room when I checked in. It was 6:40 something."

"Something?"

"Well, I don't know the time to the minute, but—"

"All right, so it was at least 6:40 when you reached your room. How long did it take you on arrival to check in?"

"Oh, I don't know, maybe ten or fifteen minutes."

"So it is possible that you and the defendant arrived somewhat before 6:30, am I correct?"

"Yes, it's possible."

Having established some uncertainty about the time of arrival, Hartwell switched to his main interest. "You rode down with the accused, Mr. Williams, right? Did you return with him?"

"No. I have family in the area. After the closing plenary on Friday, I was met by my father who drove me to my parents' place in Northford where I stayed the weekend. On Sunday, he, my father, drove me to the Amtrak station to catch the train to Boston, where I met up with an old college chum. Trying to make the most of being away from . . . from out here."

"So you did not see the accused after sometime on Friday, the 1st of March. Is that correct?"

"Yes, not after the plenary, which finished just after lunch."

"Thank you. Nothing further."

The door at the back of the courtroom opened and a man in a rumpled plaid sport coat entered and handed an envelope to one of the bailiffs. The bailiff carried it to the front and gave it to Gillian. She let out a slow exhale through pursed lips as she read the note inside.

Gillian leaned close to Brad and put her hand up to shield her mouth. "We've saved the best for last. Leave 'em laughing with a good punch line, I always say." She straighten up, stood, and turned slowly. "The defense calls its next witness: Dulce Maria Trinidade."

Hartwell objected. "She's not on your list of witnesses."

"We did not know her identity at the outset of the trial and could not locate her until now. Her testimony goes to the heart of the matter of opportunity."

"Call the witness."

Brad turned around as a petite brunette in six-inch heels entered the courtroom. He smiled broadly at her and mouthed her name: Trini.

Dulce Maria Trinidade, a Stockbridge middle-school science teacher known as Trini to her friends, had straight brown hair in a long ponytail that she flipped to the side as she took the stand. She smiled at Brad as she was being sworn in.

"Can you tell me how you know the defendant?"

"We met at the end of February, at a teachers' conference in Connecticut."

"The NEW-STEM conference?"

"Right. I wasn't even supposed to go. My girlfriend had to bail at the last minute, so I just sneaked in on her registration and hand-lettered my name badge with Trini, which is what I like to be called."

"Okay, let me ask you about Friday, the last day of the conference. Do you remember that day."

"Oh, yes." She grinned broadly.

"Could you tell us, in your own words, about that day, starting at roughly noon."

"The conference finished with a late luncheon and an after-lunch speech by a teacher who might have known how to handle ten-year-olds but did not know how to hold the attention of adults. Brad was seated next to me, and we were exchanging nasty comments about her PowerPoint slides and her 150-word sentences. There was also a poster-session in the afternoon, a last chance for the runners-up in the refereeing sweepstakes to get their moment of attention. Brad and I breezed through in fifteen minutes."

"And where did you go from there, once the conference was over?"

"Brad had requested a late checkout with the hotel, but was running out of time. He had to check out of his hotel room or be charged for another day, which he said his college wouldn't cover and he couldn't afford himself. I told him he could leave his luggage in my room, since I was already planning to stay on over the weekend.

"We dropped off his suitcase and laptop, then went out for a stroll before dinner. The stroll became a hike as we kept talking. We ended up walking for miles. Eventually we stumbled on this Italian café that appealed to both of us. After a leisurely meal—the saltimbocca was absolutely the best—we headed back for the hotel.

"It was very late, almost midnight, and I told Brad he shouldn't drive back home that night."

"And did he drive back then?"

"No. He stayed the night in my room."

"And when did Mr. Williams finally leave New Haven for the drive home?"

"Not until Sunday afternoon."

"So, Mr. Williams was still in New Haven from roughly noon on Friday until approximately what time on Sunday?"

"About two p.m., yes, two o'clock."

"Thank you very much. I have no further questions. Your witness."

Hartwell glanced inquiringly over at Gillian before approaching the witness stand. "So you are vouching for the whereabouts of the defendant for that entire period, from Friday noon to Sunday afternoon?"

"Yes."

"And you are certain of the defendant's whereabouts for that entire period. Isn't it possible that the defendant was gone for some part of that time?"

"No. He never left."

"Let me see if I understand this. You are testifying, under oath, that you can vouch for the defendant's whereabouts for the entire period in question, for that entire weekend?"

"I am."

"Forgive me if I am credulous, Ms. Trinidade, but how could you know?"

"Because I was on top of him."

A burst of laughter filled the courtroom, followed by the banging of the judge's gavel. "Order. I'll have order in my courtroom, or I will clear it."

Hartwell, clearly off balance, looked around, then walked back to his table and retrieved his notes before turning back to the witness.

"Are you testifying that you had carnal knowledge of the defendant on the night of March 1 of this year, that you had an affair with the defendant?"

"No, not an affair. I had a one-night stand. A long one. Actually a two-night stand. We sent out for room service." There was more laughter and gavel banging.

"Are you married, Ms. Trinidade?"

"Technically, yes. We're separated."

Hartwell looked lost. He opened his mouth as if to speak, then closed it again. He glared at Gillian and mouthed the word "You!" as he turned his back to the bench and returned to his table. "No further questions, Your Honor."

Brad leaned over and whispered to Gillian, "You set him up."

"Yup, like a duck in a shooting gallery."

Judge Musselman looked disapprovingly in their direction. "Any redirect, Counselor?"

Gillian stood. "No, Your Honor. The defense rests."

There were looks of surprise and quick whispers around the room.

"Well enough. This court stands recessed until ten o'clock tomorrow morning for summations." Musselman gaveled the court into recess.

Brad stood slowly. "Wasn't that a risky move? What if Hartwell had not stepped into your little pile of poo?"

"I could have asked on redirect. It wouldn't have been as dramatic or as much fun, but it would have done the job."

"That's it?"

"Yes, you always leave the audience with a good punch line. This is what will stick in the jury's minds."

"And that's what you want them to remember, that I was banging the local school marm?"

"No, that you couldn't have done it. You couldn't have killed the girl. You were otherwise occupied. This is an absolutely believable alibi from an unimpeachable source. Ba-da-boom ching!"

Brad was still shaking his head in disbelief. "But it makes me look like a real sex fiend."

"It makes you look normal. She's almost your age, recently separated, attractive, no kids. She couldn't possibly be lying because she would never risk her reputation as a school teacher making up something like that. That's how they will look at it."

"It's going to cost her."

"Probably. And most likely she hasn't realized that yet. She's still thinking Boston not the Berkshires. But she's young, resilient, she'll recover."

"But she'll probably lose her job."

"No she won't. If the school board tries to dump her, I'll take them on. The most likely thing is she'll resign in exchange for enthusiastic letters of recommendation and the promise of endorsement when her references are checked."

"You used her. And the prosecutor."

"That's what we do, what it's all about. Whatever it takes to mount the best defense for the client, guilty or not."

"You're not . . . upset over Trini?"

"You're a big boy. Who you screw is none of my business, as long as you are not screwing cheerleaders or Girl Scouts."

"But . . ."

"It's over. Forget it. I need to go work polishing my closing. Hartwell is going to hammer the jury with shock and awe, recounting the testimony from his parade of witnesses, and reviewing his catalog of forensic evidence. I don't even have a defendant to fall back on. This is going to have to be good."

"Are you anxious?"

"Not about me, not about my summation. I worry about the jury. It ends up in their hands, and no one ever knows until the foreman reads the verdict. Get some sleep, Brad."

"You, too."

"Don't be a comedian. I'll pick you up at nine. And wait until you hear my summation tomorrow. Remember, I go last."

twenty-five

HARTWELL'S CLOSING REMARKS were as predicted. He opened big, making sure that the jury remembered the seriousness of the crime and would not forget the grisly pictures of the victim's body. He centered his argument for conviction on the transcript of the online conversation, supported by the other files found on Brad's computer. "The accused abused his position of trust as a teacher. He was a tutor, the victim was his student. He lured her to her death through an online conversation that has been completely documented.

"The defense would have you believe that the accused was 'otherwise engaged' at the time of the murder. However, the confidence of the Coroner aside, the time of death is uncertain. It is merely an estimate based on what the Coroner himself admitted was inexact science. Furthermore, the accused's alibi is based on the testimony of a single witness, a witness produced at the last moment claiming to be with the accused for the entire period in question."

Hartwell finished with his characteristic punchy sentence structure. "You cannot bring that poor girl back to life. You cannot undo the evil that has been done. But you can do something. You can make sure that the man who molested and murdered her—that man sitting over there—spends the rest of his life in jail."

Gillian placed herself squarely in front of the jury before beginning.

"I am going to be even more brief than my colleague, because, as we have already shown, the defendant, Bradley James Williams, could not possibly have committed the crime with which he is charged—falsely accused.

"It was, indeed, a terrible thing, what happened to that girl. There is no doubt about that, and the prosecution has made this graphically clear. The prosecution has laid out for you an array of evidence that they claim links the defendant to the grisly murder of that poor young girl. The problem with their case is simple. Bradley Williams had nothing to do with that girl's death. He could not possibly have killed her. The only evidence that the Prosecution claims connects my client to this crime, the transcript of an incriminating online conversation, is evidence that cannot be trusted. If it can be trusted, then it conclusively exonerates the defendant. Why? If the transcript is a true and correct record of an online session, then it could not possibly involve my client. At the time indicated on that record, he was driving in heavy traffic on the way to New Haven. There was an eyewitness who testified that he made no use of his computer while driving on the freeway. For that website transcript to be linked to my client, it would have to have been falsified or altered in some way by someone. You cannot have it both ways. Either it proves the defendant was not the person who lured the victim to her death or it is false evidence that cannot be trusted.

"Even more importantly, the Defendant could not possibly have committed this terrible, terrible crime for the simple reason that he was otherwise occupied, with an alibi supplied by a member of the community who, at the risk of her own reputation, testified that he was with her for the entire period that the County Coroner said was the time of death. Someone killed that girl and mutilated her body.

But it was not Bradley Williams. Bradley Williams may be a sinner, but he is not a murderer. He is guilty only of having helped a student with her mathematics.

"There is far more than a shadow of doubt in this case. You have no choice but to find the defendant not guilty on all counts."

◊

Less than two hours had passed when Hartwell came striding from the other end of the hall with a suppressed smile poised on his lips. "The jury's back."

Brad looked at Gillian in panic. "I thought that the longer the jury is out, the better it is for the defense."

"Don't borrow trouble," she told him. "It doesn't mean anything."

"But you said . . ."

"I said a lot of things, but this is a smart jury. Maybe they reached the right conclusion quickly."

"Maybe they did at that, Counselor. After you." Hartwell gestured.

"Don't gloat prematurely, Hartwell. Don't gloat at all. It's not over."

"Ah, but I hear the fat lady warming up her vocal chords. Let's go hear her solo."

◊

Brad tried to slow his breathing and keep from shaking as Judge Musselman spoke. "Madam Foreman, has the jury reached a verdict."

The chubby former schoolteacher straightened her back. "Yes, we have, Your Honor."

"The defendant will rise. Madam Foreman, please hand the verdict to the bailiff."

When he received the folded paper, Musselman read it, stone-faced, and handed it back to the bailiff, who returned it to the foreman to read.

"On the first count, indecent assault of a minor under the age of eighteen, how finds the jury?"

"We find the defendant not guilty, Your Honor."

"On the second count, aggravated sexual assault, how finds the jury?"

"We find the defendant not guilty, Your Honor."

"On the third count, murder in the first degree, how finds the jury?"

"We find the defendant not guilty, Your Honor."

Brad covered his eyes and let the tears dribble down his cheeks, tears of relief and tears of loss. Gillian put her arm around his shoulder as District Attorney Hartwell congratulated her.

"You still have it, Gillian," he said. "You handled that extremely well. You set me up with that Trinidade woman, and I walked right into it. Well done." He held out his hand. Gillian took it without taking her left arm from around Brad.

part three: deduction

twenty-six

GILLIAN SHIFTED HER HEAD to get a glimpse of Brad in the rearview mirror. "Why so pensive? You're going home." His silence on the ride back from the courthouse was unexpected. "Didn't you hear the foreman read the verdict? Not guilty. Not guilty on all counts. We won. You won."

"No, you won. You were amazing. You won, just as I knew you would. I lost. I lost everything."

"I don't know what you are talking about. It's over, end of story."

"But with a tragic ending."

"Yes, I suppose, that poor girl."

"That poor girl had a name: Reggi. Regina Bellingham. And, the verdict notwithstanding, I was guilty on one of the three charges. And, truth be told, I . . . I loved her."

"You what?" Without realizing she was doing it, Gillian let up on the gas. "You lied to me."

"No, I said I didn't kill her. I didn't. That is what I told you. I told you no lies. I also told you that you could not put me on the stand. You assumed it was because of the divorce mess, but this is why. I didn't want to be trapped into lying on the stand."

"So, let me guess. It was the first charge: indecent assault of a minor." He nodded. "And you are telling me you what? You loved her? Is that what you call fucking a teenager?"

"You have to understand—"

"No, I don't have to understand." Her voice rose. "I thought you were this nice guy caught up in a mess, the target of inept and overzealous police work and a backcountry prosecutor out to make his reputation on the big stage. Now I find out you are some creepy pedophile who preys on young girls. I ought to make you get out here and walk the rest of the way back to town."

"Do it then."

She slowed the car even more, but before stopping, accelerated again.

He twisted in his seat to face her. "Okay, then listen to me. I really do have to tell you, because somebody did kill her. And that killer is out there. And maybe this is not the only time."

"Then let the police handle it. They aren't going to close the case just because you got off."

"Right. Let them handle it. Like they did in my case."

"You're not thinking of turning amateur detective and tackling this case yourself, are you?" She glanced at him in the rearview mirror. "No, I can see you are."

"Not alone. I can't do this alone. That's why you have to know the whole story."

"I don't have to and I don't want to." She bit off the words in sharp, separate syllables. "And I certainly have no intention of getting caught up in some quixotic pursuit of justice just to salve your conscience."

"It was not like you think. I did not take advantage of her. And we even waited until after her birthday."

"Like Elvis? Gracious God, spare me. She was just a kid."

"She was eighteen. That is what she told me."

"You're demented as well as perverted."

"She was a senior in high school."

"She was not quite seventeen, as you now know. She started school a year early, then skipped fifth grade and went directly into middle school."

"She said . . . her birthday . . . anyway, we celebrated it. Two-two-two, February twenty-two, easy to remember, she said."

"Then she lied. To please you, most likely. She was seventeen years old, sixteen when you met her. She was underage, and you were in a so-called special relationship, in a position of authority. It's a damn good thing you didn't take the stand. If this had come out . . . You're still vulnerable, you know. You were found not guilty of murder, indecent assault, aggravated assault; there could be fresh charges."

"I know, but there is no conceivable way the case could be made unless I confessed."

"You just did."

"You are still my attorney."

"Oh, God, I don't believe this." She slapped her hands on the steering wheel.

"You have to help me track down who killed Reggi."

"You keep saying that. But why? Why do I have to do anything. This is somebody else's problem. Maybe it's yours, but maybe not. It's just not mine."

"It's your problem because of who you are. You could pull over right here and let me walk back to town, but you won't. And you won't let go of it. You know something is wrong, and you know you can help me make it right. You won't leave it alone. In that, at least, we are alike."

"Damn you, Bradley Williams. When did you get so smart about me?"

"When you let us become friends." Gillian bit her lower lip and said nothing. "Now, let me tell you the whole story," he said, "because that's where we have to start, with what we know. Some-place in there are the buried signposts that will point us down the right road. No one else is going to do this; it's up to us."

"Okay, but please spare me the details."

"No, the devil is in the details. I don't know what might be impor-tant. Anyway, as I said, it was not like what you think. There was on-ly once, the third time we met, and she was the one who took the initiative. We celebrated her birthday—what I thought was her eigh-teenth birthday—a day late, and then—"

"Stop, stop. I really and truly don't want a blow-by-blow re-counting of how you acted out your middle-age sexual fantasy."

"Then just listen. Maybe you don't need to hear this. Maybe I need to tell it, to someone. Anyway, it was her idea."

"That's what every sexual predator I ever prosecuted said, the same self-serving crap. 'She really wanted it. She actually started the whole thing.' Or 'he' if the perp was into boys."

"I know, I know, but please listen. I told her no, that it wasn't go-ing to happen, that it was impossible. She said that she wanted, just once, that it not be like the other times. She told me she knew me as a soft and caring person. That was her word, soft. Ironically pre-scient, as it turned out."

"Are you saying . . .?"

"Just wait. Listen. In any case, she was not a virgin."

"As if that excuses—"

"Nothing. It excuses nothing. I am not making excuses. If any-thing, I blame myself for her death. I may not have killed her, but somehow I was involved. In a way I do not even know yet, I led her to her death, and . . . I owe her this at least: to find her killer.

"Anyway, I don't know about her other experiences. She didn't talk about them and I didn't pry. Perhaps I should have, then we might have more to go on."

"You. You might have more to go on, Brad. I finished with this case today in court." She turned on the radio and started pushing the station-search button.

Brad pressed on as snippets of music popped out. "With me, well, I was the one who was scared. I was shaking, too terrified to even get it up. Don't you see? Standing in front of me is this sweet young woman, naked, a middle-age male fantasy, as you put it, and I am quaking in my socks and skivvies, limp as a dead lizard."

Gillian tried not to laugh as she turned the radio off. "I'm sorry," she said between giggles.

"Don't be. It is funny, was funny. Pathetic. She laughed, too, and apologized, too. We ended up on the futon, laughing. We talked for hours, lying there side-by-side, just talking, about dreams and logic and dumbass people we knew and what it would be like to be famous. We shared fantasies, not about sex, but about who we would like to be if we were someone else. And then she said, 'I love you,' and I started crying. I couldn't say it then. The words stuck in my throat. It was just too monumental, too crazy, too impossible, too world-shattering to admit out loud."

Brad turned toward the window and watched the dirty snow beside the highway streaming by. He swallowed, brushed ineffectually at his tears, and talked to his own image reflected in the glass. "You couldn't do it, could you, Bradley. You failed her. You couldn't, even once, give her that to carry away with her. 'I love you, Reggi.' She never got to hear it."

Gillian reached over as though to take his hand, then withdrew it. "I . . ."

"No, it's okay. I'm okay. When she climbed on top of me, she was so tiny in my arms, so terribly, terribly vulnerable, so wanting . . ."

"You don't have to go on. Maybe it's better if you don't."

"You know what I was thinking then? What an odd couple we would have been. Mutt and Jeff. She was barely five feet in flats; I'm six-one. She was eighteen and I turn thirty-seven next month. Twice her age. More than that."

"Right, more than twice, since she was only seventeen. Not even legal."

"What the hell does that mean? The day we turn eighteen we can suddenly make decisions? Before that we could only say no, then, suddenly, we can say yes. Does that make sense? When are we responsible? When can we make judgment calls? Isn't it thirteen for Jews? Did you have a bat mitzvah? Did that suddenly change things?"

"Oh, yeah, it changed things all right. I didn't have to go to Hebrew school anymore. I did sort of feel like, 'now I'm grown up'. But this is different. Twenty years different. There was twenty years difference between you two, and she was a minor."

"Right. We were doomed, doomed lovers. A silly, deluded man and a brilliant but naïve teenage girl. Juliet. Except Juliet was fourteen, and Romeo was nowhere near old enough to be her father.

"Now, looking back, it seems not so perverse as embarrassing. I made a complete fool of myself and took enormous risks. For what? Three weekends of frantic mathematical gymnastics and microwave pizza, one late afternoon of giggling and gentle lovemaking. And a girl's life. Nothing is worth that. But the rest. If we hadn't been so isolated, off the map, in our own parallel universe, I would have been mortified by it all, blushing crimson the whole time. What a pathetic figure I cut."

"No, that's you punishing yourself—unfairly, I think. You said it. You were in love. People in love act stupid, say and do stupid things."

"You do understand."

"No, I don't understand. My definitions of things don't admit the possibility of the relationship you had. Your definitions do, apparently. It was real, I guess. Probably a very different reality for her, but also real, perhaps, as real as her experience would allow."

He turned back to the window. "Well, we're here, next right. Slow down. That corner can be tricky."

"I've been to your place before."

"I know. But that was walking, not driving."

She pulled over to the curb. "How is it that you are back in the apartment, anyway? I thought you would still be camping out with Armand."

"I was, but it wasn't working. He and Steve, his partner—it's official now—are both compulsive neatniks. I am not. But you knew that. Anyway, after a few weeks, Armand negotiated with Mrs. Hathaway for a reduction on the rent and started paying it himself. He considered it an investment in sanity. Just until I am back on my feet, he said. So, now that I am not wearing an ankle bracelet, I can move back in. And I have to try to get a job again.

"And here we are. Can you come in? We can keep talking."

"Not sure I want to keep talking. I can only digest so much at one sitting. Besides, people might talk. People, as in your pretty proselytizer from across the street, who is peeking through the curtains even as we talk."

Brad put a finger to his chin. "Speaking of talking, I just realized, it's Thursday. I have been so caught up in the trial that I forgot about the Club. Want to swing back downtown?"

"No. I've had a big day . . . a big week. I'm not up for that."

"Well, if you change your mind . . . I'm going to change out of my defendant's clothes and then head over there."

◊

Brad was not sure what to expect when he finally walked into the Muffin and Mug. Word of the trial outcome had spread quickly around town, and the place was filled with more than just the usual crowd. Four of the round tables had been shoved together in a trapezoid, a close packing now surrounded by nearly a dozen people seated and even more standing shoulder-to-shoulder. Armand, who must have come directly from the courthouse after the verdict, sat at the apex, looking like he was holding court. Next to him, an empty chair awaited. As Brad approached, Armand stood and started clapping, a slow, steady beat that took time to be picked up by others but then spread steadily around the room until everyone was clapping and most were standing.

Brad grinned and choked up as he made his way through the crowd to the empty chair. He stood behind it and nodded his thanks in rhythm with the claps. From somewhere, a tall glass of iced coffee appeared in front of him. He sat down, took a sip, and the room hushed.

It was Armand who spoke first. "Please, no speeches. But welcome back, Brad. Welcome back." He raised his mochachino frappe in a toast that brought on ragged cries of "Hear, hear!" and "Welcome back!" and shouts of "No speeches! No speeches!"

As if the Club had never adjourned or been without Brad's presence, as if he had never been on trial for murder, the group fell into a lively discussion of Guilt and its uses, of Innocence in its many guises, and a dead-on-arrival attempt by the psychologist—whose name Brad still didn't remember—to steer the group into talking about Group Cohesion.

As the crowd dwindled and Mandy cleared mugs and glasses, Brad leaned toward Armand and said, "I owe you a lot."

Armand nodded. "Yes, you certainly do—more than I think you realize."

twenty-seven

"THANKS FOR COMING OVER. It just feels so good to have my own place again. I know it's not much, but . . ." Brad held open the door for Gillian.

"It's fine. I understand the home-style cooking is pretty good here, too. The short-order cook can whip up a mean frittata in twenty minutes or so."

"Sixteen. It's on record."

"What's all this?" She waved at the papers nearly covering the kitchen table.

"I'm pulling together what we know, mapping it out so we can strategize."

"I still don't know how I let myself get talked into this, Brad, but you know me, once I'm on board I stay with the train to the end of the line. So what do we have?"

"We start with who could have done it."

"Could be anybody."

"No, it could only be somebody. The faked log from the website points to the involvement of an insider—or somebody with really good hacking skills."

"You still believe the logs were faked?"

"Or at least doctored in some way. You said it in your summation last week. The log can't be correct." He picked up the stapled transcript, rolled it, and waved it like a flyswatter. "Somewhere in here, or somewhere at WesLee Systems, is a trail of breadcrumbs that will lead us back out of the woods. This is the anomaly in the evidence. It can't be real. That's the best clue we have."

"So you are saying you really didn't have that exchange with Reggi."

"That's what I said."

"You didn't try to see her one more time?"

"I didn't. I was going to—we weren't through with the proof we were working on—but I was so confused over the direction things had taken, that I was relieved to have to put it all on hold for a bit. The NEW-STEM conference was the perfect excuse to give us a break. Besides, I figured that a week or two apart would give us a chance to step back from the mathematics, get some fresh perspective on it. And on our relationship. I—"

Gillian interrupted. "Stop. We can't do this. We're just amateurs."

"You're a professional."

"I was a prosecutor, not a detective."

"And a damn smart one. Second or third smartest person I have ever known."

"So you keep saying. Someday, I'm going to make you tell me about the others you think are smarter than me."

Brad spread his arms as if to say, "Here I am." Gillian looked around for something to throw. She tossed a black metal spring clip at him, which he caught one handed and returned to her in an underhand toss that sailed past her into the sink. "Oops. But please, no violence, Counselor. We've had enough violence in the Commonwealth lately."

"Any guesses, then, Mister Newly-Minted-Private-Eye?"

"Yeah, our spiked-hair geek. I want to know a lot more about him.

He was in a perfect position to doctor the record. It might be hard to picture him as the killer, but he was right there with his fingers in the files."

"This is work for a private detective."

"No money. You know that. Were it not for the largesse of our dear Armand, I wouldn't even have a roof over my head. At least he and Steve got their half-million back."

"Isn't Armand on the Board at the website or something? Maybe he can help."

◊

Brad finally cornered Armand the following Thursday on his way from the bank parking lot to Mandy's. "You're on the Board at InStarTute, right?"

"Board of Advisors. Why?"

"I'm doing some research. I wonder if there is any chance you might get me access to some of the files."

"Research? Leave it Brad, it's over. Let the whole matter rest."

"I can't. There's a killer out there who tried to frame me. He killed a young girl, a girl who had the whole world stretching out before her and who befriended me. I owe her something."

Armand's mouth spread into a taut line as he raised a warning finger. "The answer is no. I was glad to help in your time of trial—pun intended—but there are limits. Do you have any idea what I had to do to convince Steve to put up half your bond? No. Just leave it alone. Don't torture yourself or waste your time."

"Time is my only resource now, time and tenacity. I am not going to let go of this."

"It's your life. I just can't help you at InStartute or WesLee."

"Can't or won't."

"It's the same thing. I have an ethical responsibility to InStarTute and a fiduciary responsibility to WesLee. I went to the wall for you,

Brad. Now it's time to walk away."

Brad did a one-eighty and started back toward his apartment.

"Where are you going? It's Thursday."

"I'm walking away. I will be forever indebted to you for all that you have done, and there is no way I will ever be able even to begin to pay you back. But I am going to find out what happened and who killed Regina. Without your help, if that's what it takes."

Armand watched Brad round the corner and disappear behind the junipers at the edge of the parking lot. He reached for his cellphone and speed-dialed a number. "It's Armand here. I want you to increase physical security on the server farm, rent an extra guard or two, and get the head of IT to beef up the digital barriers, the firewall, whatever they are using now.

"No, nothing special going on, Abe. Just precautionary measures. The trial drew attention to us, which could make us stand out as a target for hackers or troublemakers. Until we are back to security through obscurity, let's not take chances. Okay?"

◊

Brad quickly learned that his technical skills were not up to anything as sophisticated as breaking into the InStarTute site to dig through files, so he and Gillian had been reduced to what they could find by searching on the Internet. They learned that Malcolm Todd was, in contrast to Brad, a consummate hacker, who had even given demonstrations at Internet security conferences on vulnerabilities in school IT systems. By purest accident, they found a reference to him as a member of a white-hat hacking fraternity calling itself Platoon EdDed. EdDed styled its work as helping school administrators secure their systems, but they had also been implicated in some grade-changing-for-money scandals. However, nothing directly tied Malcolm to the Regina Bellingham case other than some online bragging about giving testimony in court.

"It looks like we need to get inside the tutoring site and poke around."

Gillian nodded in agreement. "If he weren't our target, our Malcolm would be just the man for the job. So, who else do we know? Who hacks into computers and networks?"

"There was a friend of Regina's, a girl who went by the handle GeekGirl13. She helped Regina track me down, even got my cell-phone number. But I don't have any way of finding who she is or contacting her. I'm no longer registered on the site, and I can't risk drawing attention by trying to reapply. We need a trusted insider in some school system. I could fake a student account, but it has to be done from inside a school that is part of this consortium."

"What about your girlfriend?"

"My what?"

"How quickly men forget. She kept you out of jail a few weeks ago. Remember?"

"Trini. You're talking about the biology teacher."

"Right. Where does she teach?"

"Stockbridge, I think. Can I borrow your car? I could drive out there, but I don't even have her number."

"I do."

"Oh, yeah, right. Because she testified."

"It's in the case folder at the office. I'll email it to you tomorrow. You call her and set up a meeting. This is the kind of stuff that is best handled face-to-face, not by phone or email."

"Sure. You all right about this? I mean me contacting Trini."

Gillian shrugged and extended her lower lip. "Sure. Why not? She might be able to help. Worth a try."

◊

Brad took Exit 2 off the Mass Pike and headed for Stockbridge where he turned south on US 7 toward the Monument Valley Regional

Middle School. It was nearly five when he arrived at the sprawling, white-trimmed brick building in its immaculate and expansive setting. Trini was still waiting at the main entrance, as she had promised. She slipped him past the office and ushered him into a classroom papered with charts and posters.

"This is my office, shared, of course, with two other teachers and a hundred sixth, seventh, and eighth graders." Before Brad could say anything, she turned, stood on tiptoes, and kissed him.

"What was that for?"

"A middle school welcome for someone I am glad to see."

"I can tell."

She kissed him again. "So, what is this really about, Brad? I got the feeling that after the trial you really didn't want any reminders of that whole deal. That's what I told myself after you shook hands with me and bowed slightly as you thanked me following the verdict."

"I'm sorry. I didn't know what to say. It's a recurring problem of mine. Like right now."

"Look, it was a no strings weekend. I'm a big girl. I didn't expect it to go anywhere. But, after, well, the trial . . ."

"Are you okay? Still welcome here?"

"Oh, I get the odd look of disapproval now and then, but our Principal has been great. She thinks what I did was—what did she call it?—noble, daring."

"Your principal has been great, and I have been a jerk not contacting you."

"I figured you would when the time was right. But your phone call sounded like you want something specific, and I have this hunch it's not a reprise on our lost weekend."

"No, at least not now. I want to use one of your computers."

"You still don't have your computer back?"

"No, that's not it. I need a computer with the right IP address, one inside a school that is part of the MassAdvantage Alliance."

Confusion spread on her face, then she opened her mouth in a wide 'ah.' "I get it. You are playing detective. For a moment there I was wondering if maybe you really do stalk teenage girls. Just a moment."

"No, I prefer women who are a little older. But I need to set up an account on a website. Is that okay? As soon as I'm through, I'll wipe the account. You and the school will be fine."

"If you're doing what I think you are, you'll need a valid student ID from here." She opened the center drawer of her desk and pulled out a plastic laminated sheet. "Here, try this one, Billy Nordstrom. Copy down his ID. It's safe to pressgang him. He is one kid who would never go near a math website."

"Thanks. Can I use that computer over there?"

"Help yourself. Any chance you could stay for dinner?"

"No, sorry. I really have to get right back."

"It was fun, you know."

"Yeah. It was."

"And I am glad I could help. I wish . . ."

"Who knows . . ."

"Okay, go ahead, do your stuff. I have to check something in the library."

Brad established the account with the handle Billiant4, then deleted the browser history and shut the computer down. In the hall, Trini was just coming out of a door on the other side. She did a quick brush at her face as if flicking away a fly, but Brad could see the glistening in the corners of her eyes. He felt like a jerk.

On the drive back, he started wondering about how easily he had passed up on the opportunity Trini was offering. It was as if he were already moving on from one phase in his life but still uncertain about what was the next phase.

◊

Brad had to be coy about connecting with GeekGirl13, so it took several chat-room exchanges between Billiant4 and her before she agreed to "meet" via MoomBeam.

"Hi, is this Phoebe? You don't know me, but you know about me. You helped Regina Bellingham track me down."

"Ohmygod. You're that guy. Bradley. Ohmygod. It was . . . terrible, I mean, I . . . But you didn't do it, right?"

"Right, I didn't do it. That's why I need your help."

"Regina, you know she, like, told me, er, about you two. We were like sisters. She told me."

"I figured as much. Look, you were her friend, and now you have a chance to help us find who killed her."

"How?"

"I need you to hack into a computer system, install a backdoor so we can do some research."

"All right! I get it. Yes. The tute site. I can do it. No problemo."

"Be careful, cover your tracks well."

"Who do you think you are talking to, some kid? Regina was smart, but there is no firewall on the planet that can stop this geek girl. I've got some ideas. I'll get right on it. Let you know."

"That's good. You can reach me through this MoomBeam account."

"Can I ask you something?"

"Sure, go ahead."

"Are you really, like, bald?"

"Receding hairline."

"Ha, ha. Like that's different. Regina . . . like, it didn't matter to her. She said she, like, well . . . She was in love, I guess. Weird. I think . . ."

Brad waited, but she never finished the thought. "I'm thirty-six. I know that seems old to you now, but I am really ... Anyway, I do appreciate your help."

"Anytime, Bradster. That's what we called you: the Bradster. I'll beam you when I get in at the tute." Clink-a-clink. The connection dropped.

twenty-eight

GILLIAN HAD SUGGESTED they move their fledgling detective agency to her place where there was more room and a home office with whiteboards and a copier. After spending the day trying to rebuild her real estate practice, she swung by Brad's apartment to pick him up for the drive out Silver Point Road. There had been no new developments, and they rode in silence, with Brad, back against the door, studying Gillian's profile. Gillian pulled into the driveway and shut off the engine but sat, extending the silence without reaching for the door handle.

"Let me explain about Trini."

"Where did that come from? There's nothing in need of explanation. She provided the perfect and unimpeachable alibi for you. She helped get through to GeekGirl13, to Phoebe."

"It was not what you think."

"I don't know why you feel compelled to say anything. I really and truly don't care about your affair with some pretty, young biology teacher."

"It was hardly an affair, more like a one-and-a-half-night stand. I think both of us were suffering from small-town celibacy syndrome. We were away from watchful neighbors, had motive and oppor-

191

tunity, and I was handy, the nearest single divorcee. I certainly have no illusions of having been special to her."

"Look, Brad, I am saying I don't care that you went for her. She's young, attractive."

"There's that age thing again. You seem hung up on her being young, as if that were the main thing. What does it matter? Older? Younger? Whatever."

"Older women are not attractive to younger men."

"You're older, as you keep emphasizing, and still attractive."

"You make it sound like a passing grade on a mid-term exam. And there's that qualifier."

"Qualifier?"

"'Still', as if we were talking about some inevitable slide, an anticipation of that time when it is no longer true."

"Not inevitable. Of course, I don't know. I've never been older than thirty-six nor have I ever been attracted to a woman over the age of forty-eight, so I can't say what the limits of the phenomenon are. I don't know how it might work for so-called older couples. But I think it depends on who is looking at whom."

Gillian ignored or missed his choice of numbers. "You're talking like a professor, hedging your assertions, qualifying your qualifiers."

"And you sound like a lawyer. But an attractive one. No qualifier. Maybe what you say about younger men and older women is true on average, but I think love changes things."

"Ah, the romantic in you rears its pretty head."

"Look, Gillian, I want to tell you about my grandmother. She died at eighty-two, emphysema. At her funeral I stood at her open casket next to Gerry, the man she lived with for twenty years and her caretaker for more than a decade. He was the one who always checked her oxygen bottle and who pushed her wheelchair up ramps and lifted her in and out of their motorhome when she could no longer manage even just the two steps up. He was this short, skinny guy helping a woman who had been gaining a pound or so every year since she turned twenty.

"So, at the funeral, he looked down at her crumpled newsprint of a face with its bulbous nose and three chins above a neck like a turkey's wattle and shook his head. 'So beautiful. She's so beautiful, isn't she.' There was no question mark at the end. It was a statement that he expected all within earshot would confirm without a second thought. Truth? My grandmother might have been pretty when she was in her teens, and when I was in kindergarten she was beautiful to me because she was my grandma, but the old woman in the coffin in front of us was not beautiful—except to Gerry. And his was the opinion that mattered.

"Love is beer goggles for the sober and committed. Gerry might as well have been some lonely stud in a bar with three-and-a-half beers under his belt hitting on some unaccompanied woman perched on the stool next to his." Brad swept his hand down over his face, put on a crooked grin, and started to weave erratically. "What is a girl like you doing here drinking alone?" he said, slurring his speech. "You know, you're beautiful. You could have any man in the room. You could have me." He leaned unsteadily toward Gillian, stopping only inches from her face before snapping out of his impersonation.

"Gerry's love for my grandmother made her beautiful. Better than beer goggles and not as hard on the liver. She was over eighty, so I guess the word 'still' as a qualifier is not much of a hedge in your case. Gerry loved my grandmother so much that it kept him alive and it killed him. No one was surprised when he died barely six months after she did. He walked into a 7-Eleven for a pack of cigarettes and never walked out. Both he and Grandma were heavy smokers. He went up to the counter to ask for Marlboros, closed his eyes, and slumped to the floor. It was a massive heart attack, but the autopsy revealed that the attack had actually happened decades earlier; the damage to his heart just finally caught up with him. His love for my beautiful grandmother had kept him going until he was no longer needed."

"Now that, Brad, is a sweet story. But why do I think you have embellished it or selectively simplified where convenient?"

"Why? Because you're a cynic. But it's true; it happened that way." He reached for the door handle, then leaned toward her and kissed her quickly. "Thanks. Thanks for saving my life. Thanks for being there. And I, for one, think you are beautiful."

Gillian, suddenly finding the steering wheel worthy of her full attention, stared straight ahead and made no immediate attempt to leave for the house. When she looked up, Brad was standing at the driver's side. He smiled and opened the door for her. "I hope this is all right with you, Counselor, but my beautiful grandmother taught me to open car doors for ladies."

Gillian smiled back and took his hand as she got out of the car. They strolled slowly, hand-in-hand, toward the front porch. "Do you want to sit a spell, my old-fashioned gentleman? I could get us some lemonade." She winked.

"No, I want to be invited in. Then I want to be invited to stay. You see, old-fashioned but blunt."

"Direct. You can come in."

"Redirect, Counselor. What are your intentions on the matter of this invitation?"

Her smile deepened as she shook her head. "Objection. Calls for a conclusion."

"Overruled. Conclusions are called for."

"All right, then." She laughed lightly. "Let's go inside and conclude what we will."

twenty-nine

PHOEBE CALLED VIA MOOMBEAM the next day to deliver details of how
to use the backdoor access she had set up. "Most of the key files—
logs, administrative settings, user account details—are encrypted.
But these numbnuts are using a simple technique that was easy to
crack. Plus, their keys are short. And, they reuse the same passwords for a lot of things. I put a ZIP file in your Billiant4 dropbox
with all the passwords for the files I was able to crack."

"Right, okay, I see it." Brad dragged the file to his desktop and
double clicked. "It's locked. What's the password?"

"You figure it out."

"No, wait. Not fair."

"Fair. If you are as smart as you think you are, you'll get it. Anyway, once you are logged in at InStarTute, don't muck around. If you
change anything, it will get flagged and is likely to be noticed, and
next time around they will make it a lot harder to break in."

"Okay. So what are my login credentials?"

"In the ZIP file."

"Oh, no. What if I can't open it?"

"Then you suck." Clink-a-clink. She had disconnected.

Brad stared at the new file: oiler-1.zip. The clue had to be in the name of the file. oiler. But it had to be mathematical. Maybe a pun, Euler rather than oiler. Now that had possibilities. Euler's Identity, the formula that many had called the most elegant statement in all of mathematics, was the most obvious candidate. Brad wrote out the formula in the form he remembered it:

$$e^{\pi i} + 1 = 0$$

How could that be a password? And the file was oiler-1 not oiler. Euler minus one? That would be e to the πi. So, then, EPII? No, it would be lower case for the e and the i: epii? He tried both. Nothing. Okay. etothepii? Still wrong. Wait: e2thepii. Wrong again. Maybe another play on words, like oiler? He kept hammering away until the file finally unlocked with ee2thepieeye. "Oh, Phoebe, you do like to make it hard on the Bradster."

◊

Gillian looked over his shoulder. "Any luck?"

"Yes. Our Malcolm has been a naughty boy. I think we are onto something."

"How naughty?"

"Like collecting compromising webcam pictures of some of the students?"

"You're kidding."

"Nope. Look at this." He brought up a gallery of thumbnails, mostly low-resolution photos of topless young girls with a few shots of boys interspersed, one of them sporting a monster boner sticking out of his fly. "Our lad had varied tastes, that is for sure."

"Regina?"

"Not that I could find, but over in the maintenance logs I did find something. He had an extended real-time chat with her at one time, supposedly about her account being blocked. It seems to have been a ploy he used to connect with girls—and a few guys—and talk them into showing some skin. This is our man."

"A little porn doesn't make for murder one. You are making a long-jump to an unwarranted conclusion."

"Look at this, Gillian, he was collecting the stuff. Look at the dates on the files. He has been doing this for years."

"Aren't you doing the same thing the police and the DA did with you?"

"No, it's not at all the same. This guy is a pervert who has been cyber-stalking teenagers. He did it, I know it."

"This makes him a sex offender, assuming some or all of these kids are underage, but that's a far cry from making him a murderer. This is well short of what a grand jury would need to vote to indict."

"Police work, that's what you are saying it will take. We have to tie him to the crime scene, that stuff."

"Yeah. We could also turn this over to the police, who actually do that kind of work. That is, if that's how you want to play. But what if he had nothing to do with Regina? He's going to get a life sentence anyway, as you once told me about. He's, what, twenty-six? He'll do time on child porn charges, then spend the rest of his life on the Sex Offenders Registry."

"Are you now defending what he's been doing?"

"Hardly, just suggesting we get more evidence before we wreck the chances of getting the real criminal on the real crime."

"Ideas?"

"Think, Brad. What would the police do?"

"Question him."

"We could try that. You would have to do it."

Brad hung his head over the keyboard. "This is messier than I expected, but I'll try. You have his address from the trial."

"Let's do some more forensics first. Is there any way to see if he's connected with the doctored transcript?"

"There's a check-in/check-out system for all the logs. Unless he also hacked that, it might indicate if he touched the file." Brad tapped away at the keyboard for several minutes. "I found the records I needed, but that log, that day, was only accessed once the log was subpoenaed."

◊

Malcolm was just turning the key in the front door of his farmhouse when he realized there was someone waiting on the porch. He jumped. "You're . . . you're that guy."

"I'm that guy."

"What . . . what do you want?"

"Can we talk?"

"I don't know. I'm . . . kinda busy."

"Just a few minutes, that's all, I just want to ask you some questions."

"About the log transcript, right? Well, I didn't do anything with it. That was exactly how we retrieved it under subpoena. You say it wasn't you, but there it was. I don't think anyone hacked into your account."

"Let's forget about the log transcript for now. What about these files." He unfolded a sheet of thumbnail photos and held it up for Malcolm. "Recognize these?"

"Oh shit! How? How did you . . . No. Look, I never hurt anyone. I didn't hurt that girl, never even saw her. I never hurt anyone. Please."

"But you collect pictures. You like young girls. Boys, too."

"It's just, like, a hobby. I don't really do anything, just collect them, you know. Cute . . ."

"And did you ever try to pull this on Regina Bellingham?"

"I . . . Yes, I tried once. I thought she was, like, interesting, and I knew she had been . . . coming on to you, so I figured I had a chance. She shut me down, threatened to go to my boss. I'd lose my job.

Please don't say anything to my boss."

"I wasn't planning to. I was thinking of the police. They would find your collection very interesting."

"Oh, God no." He slumped down against the front door until his knees were at his chin. "Please no."

"You still claim you had nothing to do with Regina Bellingham's death, that you did not in any way change the log files—or create them?"

"I swear, I didn't do anything. I didn't hurt anyone. Trust me. I just collected pictures. You gotta believe me. You gotta." He looked up at Brad, hands folded, pleading, prayerful.

Brad backed away, then walked out to the road where he had left Armand's car.

◊

"And you believe him?" Gillian sipped the last of her cup of herb tea.

"Yeah, I guess. It is hard to picture the scared kid I talked with doing . . . doing that to Regina. But, to be honest, I cannot picture what kind of a person could do that. Cannot."

"Where does that leave us?"

"He's still on my list, but we definitely don't have enough on him. If he didn't fudge the files, who did? It had to be somebody with access, administrative privileges at the top level."

"Like Armand?"

"Yeah, someone like Armand. Hang on there. You're not suggesting . . ."

"I'm just saying. And he has tried to persuade you not to dig into this. You have said he is somewhat polymorphous perverse when it comes to sex."

"But . . . Armand. That's just not . . . It's impossible." Gillian said nothing but continued to lock with Brad's eyes. "He's my friend."

"Which makes it all the harder to think objectively."

"But why did he help me? Why wouldn't he just let me go to jail."

"Because he's your friend. Didn't he say he had good reason to believe you didn't do it? What better reason than if he knows something?"

Brad covered his face.

"Look, we just have to keep digging and go wherever the evidence leads. You want to catch whoever killed Regina. We won't be able to do that if we are ready to give everyone a free pass."

thirty

BRAD WAS LISTENING TO NPR when Gillian arrived and stood outside the screen door. "Did you hear the news?"

"What? I just turned it on."

"Local, not national. They found Malcolm in the barn at his little farmstead, dangling from a steel cable, apparent suicide. The police said there was a suicide note, but they are not releasing the contents pending notification to next-of-kin."

"Oh, my God."

She sat down at the table with him and started peeling a tangerine. "Switch stations, let see if there is anything more."

They waited through a feature on the steady increase in farmers' markets in Western Massachusetts and a report of a convenience store robbery in Holyoke. "Police have now disclosed that the suicide note left by Malcolm Muybridge Todd made reference to the recent murder of Regina Bellingham, focus of a police manhunt and a dramatic trial at which Todd had testified. Todd avowed in his note that he had nothing to do with the murder and that he had never touched anyone. Police, who found pornography on Todd's computer, are nevertheless looking into a possible link with the murder. More on this story as it develops."

Gillian reached across the table for Brad's hand, but he pulled it away. "It's not your fault."

"No, it's not my fault. Nothing is my fault. Except that what I touch dies. A brilliant young mathematician was brutally murdered and now a quirky, probably harmless, young man is dead by his own hand. No, it's not my fault."

"Brad."

"I had something to do with both of them, for one reason or another, they died because I came into their lives."

"Brad, stop it. You talked with this kid, that's all. He obviously was troubled."

"And if I talk with Armand? What then? How many people are going to die because of me? I'm a Typhoid Mary."

"That's it, Brad. I have had enough of this. If you want to take it all on and blame yourself, okay, but leave me out of your pity party."

"Good, then maybe you won't have to die, too."

"Bradley James Williams. I love you, but I wish you had one rational neuron in that over-educated cranium of yours."

"You what?"

"You are so irrational and exasperating. You—"

"No, before that. What did you say?"

"I love you, but . . ."

"Me, too, with the 'but' in there, too. I love you. But."

"But what?"

"Fill in the blank. But what are we going to do? But what about your 'I'm no cougar; I don't do younger men?' But what about Regina's killer? My scattered life? The debt I've run up? My ex-wife? My sixteen-year-old daughter? What about Armand?"

"Armand is easy. We have to talk with him. The love bit, that's hard. I don't know what to do about it. I guess we have to talk, too."

"I hope so. That's one of my two most favorite things for us to do together."

"One of two, huh?" He nodded. "I imagine I can figure the other one out. But right now, I think we have an appointment with our friend Armand Richelieu."

◊

Armand leaned over the railing of the redwood deck. "Look who's here. And the pretty lawyer in tow. Two guests for the price of one. Go back around front. I'm sorry I didn't hear the doorbell. I was talking to my potted plants, trying to convince them to grow even when I forget to water them."

Brad and Gillian followed the flagstone path back toward the front entrance and waited for Armand to appear.

"Here, come on in. Can I get you something? A lemonade? Beer?"

Gillian looked to Brad to take the lead, but he said nothing. "Sure, I'll take a lemonade."

"Brad? Nothing? Okay, go on out to the deck. You both know the way. I'll grab a couple of lemonades and meet you there."

On the deck, Armand introduced them to his potted tomato plants, each one with a name. "Steve loves this stuff, but Steve is away fourteen days a month, so I have to try and keep them all happy. That one there, Beatrice, is anal retentive, I think. A half-dozen blossoms and only three set. Those tomatoes better be damn delicious and as big as melons." He sipped his lemonade and set it down on the railing. "But you didn't come here to talk about gardening. What's on your mind, Brad?"

"Regina Bellingham."

"Still? You have to move on."

"First, I find who killed her; then I move on."

"You're not real good at taking advice, are you. Let the police do their jobs."

"Have you been questioned by the police since the trial?"

"No. Why?"

"Because if you recall, a key piece of evidence was a doctored or falsified transcript originating at WesLee, which hosts the InStar-Tute website. The inconsistencies have never been explained."

"We turned over our documents to the police during the original investigation. That's all I know. If they are working on that transcript, I wouldn't know; they certainly haven't approached me about it."

"Do you have any idea how the transcript could have been faked or changed? I mean, who inside could pull off something like that."

"Nobody, if I believe my IT people. The whole system is set up to keep track of every access, every change. The system's an adaptation of the techniques used in medical record keeping. There's a tracking entry made whenever anyone touches any of the files on our hosted websites. That was part of why we were chosen for InStarTute and a number of other sites."

"Even a clever technician couldn't get around the system?"

"If you are thinking about that programmer, you're too late. The poor kid. Somebody got to him. My guess is they threatened to expose his cyber-stalking hobby."

"You knew about that?"

"Not everything, not until it came out in the news. But even if I had known, the most I would have done would be to quietly fire him and urge him to get help. As far as I can see, he never hurt anyone, although everyone is now eager to link him to Regina's death. It would be nice closure, wouldn't it? The dangerous stalker and vicious killer is now dead. Case closed. Except it doesn't wash. He was just a young man with slightly off-center sexual tastes who liked to project pictures on his bedroom wall and jerk off. Basically, a nice kid."

"You talk as if you knew him."

"I did. We fooled around some when he first came to work for WesLee."

"You were lovers?"

"For a bit. But we both tired of it. No, this kid could not possibly have killed the girl. He was afraid of his own shadow. He had a job that kept him in darkened rooms in front of a screen, safe, away from the sun or living people. He liked pictures, especially pictures of girls with firm little tits or boys with big boners. He was not very good with the real thing."

"What I don't understand is why you don't—didn't—want me digging, you know, digging into WesLee."

Armand leaned away from them. "Are you thinking I belong on your suspect list?"

"You are known for being . . ."

"Lustful? An epicure of the exotic? And that makes me a murderer?"

"No, but you had privileged access to the InStarTute files, which gives you opportunity to falsify—"

"Get out!"

"What?"

"You heard me. Get off my property. That's it. I've had it with you both."

thirty-one

GILLIAN STOPPED THE CAR at the bottom of the driveway. "I still don't think it's Armand. Besides, we have nothing, not even circumstantial evidence, to link him to the murder."

"You don't think his pyrotechnics were not covering up something?"

"Maybe. But maybe nothing to do with Regina. Do you mind if I go back in and try to talk with him?"

"What makes you think he'll talk with you but not with me?"

"Because I'm not you, not male. Let me give it a shot.

"Sure. It's your fune . . ."

Gillian got out of the car. "I sure hope not," she said, shaking her head as she trudged back up the driveway.

Armand answered the door on the first ring. "I thought I told you—"

"It's me, Gillian. We're friends, remember? I just want to talk a minute."

Armand stood with his arms crossed but stepped back to let her in. "This is a non-starter. I already told you the transcript was not, could not have been messed with. And it wasn't me."

"Then what's up? Why this stiff-arming your friends?"

"Christ on a crutch, I told you."

"Then why do you keep discouraging us from digging at WesLee."

He sighed deeply as he paced. "Okay. What the fuck, you might as well know. But you have to swear this stays here. You can tell Brad because if you don't he'll keep gnawing away at it until he really messes things. So this has to stay in our small circle. Okay?"

"What exactly is 'this'?"

"I don't want anyone looking too close at WesLee or InStarTute because I have been doing some creative accounting. With the economic downturn, we started running into some cash-flow problems. I just need a little more time. Steve's helping me. He set up a few sham websites that are paying premium prices. By the end of the year, we should have enough to make everything look right. Then I can repay the 'loans' from the non-profit sites we manage, and . . ."

Gillian smiled. "I believe you. You have reminded me of what my dad used to say."

"What's that?"

"If they don't have their hands in somebody's pants or up a skirt, they probably have them in the till."

"Your dad was a cynic."

"And proud of it. Raised me well." She started toward the door. "Thanks, Armand. I should go and tell Brad."

◊

In the car, she passed on what Armand had told her. "So, now we know. But, you realize where this leaves us, Brad?"

"Heading out without a clue again."

"We had a way of working on such cases when I was with the DA. If we lost the trail or none of the leads panned out, we went back to the victim and worked our way out from there. We should see what Regina Bellingham might have to tell us."

◊

It was too early in the season to start the furnace, so Brad had laid a fire in the living room fireplace to take the chill off. Gillian motioned him to join her on the couch, then slid the manila folder on the coffee table toward him. "So, that's the stuff I could find out about her background. Regina's mother, Talia Diamond Josephson, got pregnant out of wedlock, she raised her daughter as a single parent for ten years. They started out in Newton Lower Falls, so at first they must have been doing all right, family money or something, but they ended up in public housing, scraping by, with the mother working as a domestic sometimes, sometimes on welfare, maybe doing tricks. My pals back at the DA's office found some priors, nothing big: shoplifting, possession, soliciting. One year she marries Jonathan Bellingham, a construction worker. It must have been stormy from the outset. Records show repeated domestic disturbance calls. Then, one day, she disappears. Missing person report filed by the husband, but she is never found. Nothing, not a trace."

"Do we know anything about Reggi's father?"

"Regina's birth certificate names the father, but the copy I saw had it redacted. It might be possible to get a copy of the original, with the right reason or the right incentive. Another formal murder investigation, if it ever came to that, could shake it free."

Brad closed the slim folder. "Reggi never talked much about her family. If I brought it up, she'd just change the subject. She was focused outward, dreamed about getting out, away to college. Stanford had accepted her, but then she met me and started talking about going to Brandeis instead, to stay closer. I told her I'd follow her to California. God, was I ever stupid. We didn't have a future. I couldn't have followed her to California, and she would have soon met someone her own age. How could I have been so . . . so . . . I was sometimes as naïve as she was. We were in some parallel reality where Jerry Lee Lewis would not be treated as some kind of pervert because he marries his fourteen-year-old cousin.

"I still can't get used to the fact that Reggi was actually so young. The Reggi I knew seemed like most kids about to graduate from high school, convinced they are already grown up and ready to take on the world."

"Maybe she was. Kids grow up at different rates—and faster these days. She was a senior. That had to have some effect on her, being surrounded by older kids all the time. She would have been thinking like a kid about to leave home for college. But she got derailed, involved with . . . an older man."

"Now you're making it my fault." He stood, then walked to the other side of the coffee table.

"You're the one who overstepped the line." She looked up at him.

"The line? There you go again, as if an entire relationship were defined by sex. Is that what we are about, you and I. Is that the defining feature of our life as . . . as a couple, that we have intercourse?"

"No, that's not what I mean. It's more than that, of course, a lot more." She joined him in the middle of the room.

"But you are prepared to define my relationship with Reggi based on that. Yes, we made love. Once. We also spent months exchanging IM notes on mathematics, we spent long hours talking about music and what it means to love someone, and we compared the poetry in the lyrics of Phil Ochs and Denton Reynolds. We spent days and days working almost around the clock in a frenzy of flip-chart diagrams and symbolic expressions, arguing, trying to finish something of significance, of lasting importance. We ate microwave pizza at two in the morning and typed revisions to her proof at three. We watched the sun rise over the mountain and laughed over instant coffee. And we made love—had sex, if you prefer—for how long? Twenty minutes? Twenty-five, tops. How does that define our relationship? Why is that the single most important thing?"

He looked off into the distance. "You know, I couldn't even tell you the shape of her breasts. I—"

"Oh, please."

"No, really. I don't remember whether her navel was an innie or an outie."

"Brad!"

"But I can tell you about the way her dark eyes widened when she was getting an idea. I can remember the way her dimples deepened, even without a smile, when she liked one of my arguments. And I can hear her voice, always husky but becoming hoarse as the hours of work dragged on, as she thanked me for helping, for helping with the math."

"Fine. Noble you. But you fucked her."

"Okay. I did. Call it what you want. Maybe it was all wrong. I confess, I simply do not know. I'm in no position to judge. Clearly, you are. And I am making no excuses, no defense, Your Honor."

"Not fair, Brad."

"Probably not. Sorry. But all I am saying is that this was one small thing, a single, brief event in something much bigger and more complicated."

"So it was nothing. You think that makes it all right? I think that makes what you did all the more wrong. It was nothing, nothing important, no big deal. To you, maybe."

"No, it was a big deal. It was beautiful. That's the God-loving truth, Gillian. It was sweet and special. Afterwards, as I drifted in and out of sleep and she kept talking, she told me that it was the only time, that the other times didn't count, that I was the first, the first to make love to her."

"Like a virgin, touched—"

"Shut up!" It was a shout like a close-by lightning strike that left Gillian with her mouth open and her eyes wide in shock.

"I'm sorry." He reached toward her, both hands open in supplication.

"Don't touch me," she snarled. "Don't you yell at me, and don't you touch me. I took this from Carl for sixteen years, and I won't ever again take it from any man."

Brad lowered his hands and turned away. "The fire is going down. I'll put another log on." He busied himself with the poker, knocking loose embers from the logs, then positioning a fresh log at an angle on top. When he turned back, Gillian's eyes dropped to the poker still in his hand. He laid it on the hearth, slowly, carefully, like a gunfighter surrendering to authorities, never taking his eyes from her face.

"We have problems," he said, his voice just above a whisper. "Big problems." He took a step toward her, and she took a step back. "I'm not Carl."

"And I'm not Regina."

Brad's eyes narrowed and his mouth opened slightly, as if he were working on a math problem and sketching the mental edges of a possible solution. "No, you're not. It goes back to trust, that and . . ."

"No, you got that right. I am not some trusting teenager."

"Neither was she, after what she had been through. No, she was not trusting, but she trusted me. You don't."

She looked him straight in the eye. "No."

The hiss and crackle of the fire filled the long silence. "It's not just me," Brad finally said. "Your problem is that you just do not do trust." He spaced the last words, giving each a soft punch, like a muffled drumbeat.

"Don't psychoanalyze me, Bradley. You don't know me well enough to make a blanket statement like that."

"How well do I have to know you to say it? How long before I am allowed to say it, simply and flatly? You don't trust. Not anyone."

Her eyes narrowed in anger, but she said nothing.

"I, however, trust you," he said.

"Which is easy for you. Because you—"

"Easier, perhaps. Not easy."

"—are a man. It's always easier for men. Less at risk. Easier if you are younger, too."

"So, I qualify on two counts, on gender and age. Okay, I'll do the trusting for both of us. I'll tell you what I haven't said before. I'll trust you with everything: the secrets I have never spoken aloud, the truth, the whole truth." As he was talking, he had been inching toward her. With less than two feet separating them, he placed his hands straight at his sides, and stood, unmoving, silent.

Her eyes darted around his face, and she looked anxiously down at his arms. He said nothing, did nothing, until she leaned forward, almost imperceptibly.

"I love you, Gillian. I love you whether you trust me or not."

She raised an arm and closed her hand into a fist. "Damn you, Bradley Williams. Why did you do this? Why did you have to mess up my life?" She took a step and struck him on the shoulder, not violently but not entirely playfully.

"Aaaah!" He cringed. "Not my bum shoulder. If you must use violence, batter the other side."

She lowered her head, laughing through tears. He awkwardly bent over, twisted his face upward, and kissed her lightly. She took his face in both hands and kissed him back with passion. "And I love you, too. And I will probably live to regret it, and to regret ever saying it. You are probably going to dump me for a younger woman before I even get used to having you in my life."

Brad straightened up and stretched his back. "I'm the one who's feeling old right now. No younger woman would have me, what with being well on my way to premature baldness. Then there's my bad shoulder earned biking in Cambridge and my bad back, wholly unearned. Now, throw in my apparent inability to handle even the most elementary erotic acrobatics."

"Erotic? Acrobatics? Bending over to kiss me?"

"Well, twisting over and up to kiss you."

"Listen, mister, you have not seen anything yet."

"But I am looking forward to it. And I am not going to dump you. Not for a younger woman or an older one."

"How can I trust that from a man who consorts with adolescents?"

"And now we are truly getting somewhere, to the dark heart of the matter." He spoke with mock drama in his voice.

"What are you talking about?"

"You. Regina. You need to realize that there is absolutely no need to feel threatened."

"Threatened? Are you kidding? She's . . ."

"You were going to say she's dead. Like I said, no need to feel threatened."

"But there could be another Regina."

"Never. She was one of a kind, a beautiful, brainy, adolescent prodigy, a girl genius from a small town out East with a million-dollar dream."

"That's not what I meant. There are other young girls. Young women."

"Who are not you and are not Regina."

"But they have flat tummies and firm tits."

"And long blond hair. Or red, if the gentleman prefers. So what? I told you, I don't even remember her tits."

"I do. I saw the pictures. She was seventeen and had bigger boobs than I have. Had. Ever."

"You can't base a relationship on a pair of breasts. I want a relationship."

"Then you better be ready for it, young man, because you are never going to get much in the breast department from me."

thirty-two

"HOW DID YOUR BEAM CALLS go, Sherlock?"

Brad put his elbows on the table and his chin on his fists. "Meh. All I could learn from our geek girl was how smart Reggi was, how much she despised her family, how besotted she was with me, and how certain she was that she could win the Millennium Prize. Nothing new, and not much to go on."

"No, not much. It's too bad we can't get ahold of Regina's computer. It might have something we can use. I know this guy who does hard-drive forensics who could probably recover erased files from it."

"Well, we can't get ahold of her computer, not unless you are ready to add breaking and entry and theft to your CV."

"Grand larceny. If the computer is worth enough."

"Whatever. But we don't need her computer, and there probably isn't anything on it, anyway. Reggi was really careful—and smart. We never sent emails but instead left messages as drafts in a Gmail account we shared. She only used computers at the library or the high school, so there would be no trace on her own computer. If it were of possible relevance, Reggi would have uploaded it."

"Did you check to see if there was anything there?"

"No, not since the mess started. Back then I didn't want to tip off the police. I figured everything I was doing was being noted. But now, why not?" He logged into leon.bigollo@gmail.com, their shared account, and started poking around. "There's her last message to me, still in the Drafts folder. You can read it, if you want. She said she was still working on this one step in her proof and couldn't wait to get back with me.

"Wait. Here's something odd. There's a file in the recycle bin, called pisano.doc." He dragged it out and tried to open it. "It's corrupted. Or it's not a .DOC file. Maybe it's compressed." He copied and renamed the file with a .ZIP extension. When he double clicked, he got a message asking for the password.

She patted him on the shoulder. "Aren't you clever. Now we just have to figure out the password. Or get some cracking software to do it for us."

"I am pretty sure what it is, or at least what sort of thing it is."

"How?"

"Because she was a math nut. The file name is related to the account name. That's short for Leonardo Pisano Bigollo, the mathematician."

"Never heard of him."

"Sure you have. Fibonacci? Same guy. The passphrase for this account is fibonachos. She wanted to use Fibonacci, but I said it was too easy to guess. So pisano.zip has to be related to Fibonacci. Knowing her, she probably would have used numbers; she wanted to use 1123581321 as the password for email."

"What's the significance of that?"

"The Fibonacci series: 1, 1, 2, 3, 5, 8, 13, 21, and so on. Each term is the sum of the preceding two terms."

"Why didn't you use that?"

"Again, too easy to guess if you knew who Leonardo Bigollo was, which would be easy enough to find out from the Wikipedia. Plus, you have to have some letters in the password."

"She wouldn't have used the same password as the email account, would she?"

"No, she was too clever and devious for that, but I'll try it anyway." A beep and a "wrong password" message confirmed Brad's hunch.

"Let's see. She would have used something trickier, once removed. Maybe the limit, the golden ratio."

"What?"

"The ratio of successive terms of the Fibonacci series converges on one-half of one plus the square root of five. It's called the Golden Ratio or Golden Mean because the ancients considered it the perfect proportion for shapes. It's also called phi, and it's approximately 1.618."

"So let's try it."

"The password has to start with at least one letter. We could write it out. One-point-six-one-eight." He tried various ways of entering the number; none of them worked. "There are just too many possibilities. Let's try 'goldenratio.' Nope. Okay, 'goldenmean.' Nope."

"What did you call it?"

"Phi, the Greek letter phi. Phi is approximately one point—"

"Type that in."

"No, it can't be 1.61803 etcetera. It has to start with letters."

"But it's not 1.618 whatever. Didn't you say she was a stickler for precision? Type in phi, just as you said it to me."

He typed "approximately1.618" into the password box, and the folder opened, exposing several files. Gillian reached past him to double-click on the file named BJW.jpg. A headshot of Brad popped up.

"It's my faculty snap from when I was teaching at Brandeis. Before the fall, the divorce. I had more hair."

"Look at the date on the file. You were right. She was stalking you."

"Too strong a word, more just very curious. I told you, she tracked down my name and cellphone number. Smart and determined, she wanted to know everything. Let's see what this next JPEG is." Brad double-clicked pickupx.jpg. A map popped up, a satellite view with a red, tear-drop-shaped "pushpin" at the center that marked the image as coming from GoogleMaps. There were no labels, and the copyright claim and scale had been cropped off. Most of the area was wooded, with a few thin roads slicing through. What might have been a winding dirt track ended at the site of the pushpin.

"This must mean something, if it was as important to her as your photo. But it could be anywhere."

"But it's not. It's somewhere. We'll just have to figure it out eventually. Let's look at the document. Strange name. I wonder what would be in a file called Tumi.docx."

The title page revealed the secret: To Me: A Diary but not Daily.

> i really want 2 do this this time. i am no good at writing. i do numbers better. but i want 2 know this stuff is somewhere besides my head. if anyone is reading this, u shouldn't. this is me, so it's mine. go away. and if u r jack i will kill u. starting with cutting off that ugly little dick of yours. u will never read anything mor or fuck anyone else. and if u r big jack, i will kill u 2 and fry your nuts in lard u lard-ass. u r 2 of a kind.

"My, the girl had violent fantasies. And a sailor's vocabulary."

"Oh, yes, my Reggi had a mouth on her. Got her into trouble more than once. Let's see. From the date of the first entry here, she would have been, what, thirteen when she started the so-called diary."

Gillian was reading over his shoulder. "You should keep reading this stuff. It's interesting."

"It's a dead girl's diary."

"Are we doing this or not, Brad? Either we are investigating or we are just playing games here. As a game, this is a little morbid; as a murder investigation it's something, well, maybe more honorable."

"Or driven. So, what does she say to herself?" He started reading the next entry. "Oh, shit!"

> it was my birthday yesterday. i'm a teenager now. good party. friends. all older, of course. good swag. earbuds. and i got the iPhone. and the special present i was not expecting. except i should of seen it coming. all the stuff b4. he fucked me. finally the real deal. it hurt. i told him no. i screamed. he covered my mouth. i tried to bite his hand. he twisted my head. i thought this is it. i'm going to die on my birthday with him on top of me. i didn't die. too bad. he got off. LOL. punny story. i didn't cry. he can fuck me, but i won't let him make me cry.

"This is not going to be an easy read. Who is this 'he'? Who raped her at thirteen? A boy from the party maybe?"

"Read on, maybe we'll find out."

"Okay, but the next one's dated over a year later.

> i hate my mother. i don't even remember her. i mean i know what she looks like. but i don't remember her, think about her, except to hate her. she married big jack. u have a brother now. a big brother. ya, big dumb brother, can't multiply, can't spell, can't remember to change his socks. her fault. she married, then she split. not a word. no goodbye, no i can't take this anymore i'm sorry pumpkin. one day she is there, one day she is not. we have to go find her, i said. big jack told the police she split because of us kids. always fighting. she'll show up in a week or so, he said. when she runs out of money for booze. my mother

didn't drink. not much. she smelled like lavender. soap.
clean. jack smells like dog shit. he rubs it on his feet.
ROFL. and changes his socks only when big jack yells at
him. i miss my mother. i turn 13 and 2 weeks later, she
bails on us. i wish i could remember her. already i can't
remember her. someday I'll find her.

"This is a big document. Do we read through in order or skip to see how it all comes out?"

"Both. Maybe we should go to some of the last entries."

Brad went to the end of the file, where the last entry started at the top of the page. It was just before Regina had disappeared.

b came back early. says he couldn't stay away, missed me. i
missed him 2. my crazy horny b. he used the tute to
message. i said we should use the gmail, he said don't
worry. he wants to meet, not at Armand's, a different place.
come out. i said i don't have a car. he said i could walk
from the bus station. he'd pick me up at this parking lot. i
can't wait to have him inside me again. tomorrow.

"You came back early? You lied to me. You said you were at the conference, in Hartford, the whole week."

"I was, I didn't lie. She's obviously referring to the phony chat. This 'b' refers to someone else."

"Yeah. Right. The fake transcript that could not have been faked. And maybe the moon is . . . Oh, shit, this is not helping."

"No it isn't. But look, you still don't have to believe me if you don't want to. Just follow the evidence wherever it leads. If it leads back to me and you have probable cause, you can turn me in yourself."

"Double jeopardy. You've already been found not guilty."

"Rightly so. I didn't kill her. You already know all about my sins. Once we have done our job, then you can turn me in for those, if you really want to. Until then, at least pretend that you believe me, because otherwise we waste a lot of time with you suspecting me or accusing me of lying and me protesting to no lasting effect. Okay?"

"Okay. But you used Armand's place? If he is an accessory, he could still be charged? What does he know?"

"He doesn't know anything; he is not an accessory. I have a key to the place. I look after it when he is away. And he leaves his car keys with me when he is off jet-setting with Steve or one of his other boyfriends. Or girlfriends. I drive him to Worcester Airport or to Hartford and pick him up on the return. I used his car and his cabin. It takes forever to thaw the place out in the winter, but once that Franklin stove really kicks in, it can get so cozy that you can sit around in the altogether while the arctic winds howl outside."

"I'll bet."

"Shall we read on?"

"That was the last entry."

"Well, we can start backwards or go back to where we left off."

"Go back."

They spent the rest of the evening reading through the terror and trivia that had been Regina Bellingham's life as a teenager. She had been sexually abused off and on over a couple of years by someone never named. The threat to go public was her power, but she had chosen not to use it.

> he knows i mean it. one move and he's toast. but i just want to hold him off until i can get away. in college. then when i get the prize, i never have 2 go home again. no foster home 4 me. my friend donna clued me in. no way. i just keep the threat on him. hold on another year. graduation.

"It's gotta be Jack or Big Jack."

Brad rubbed his eyes with bunched fingers. "My money's on Big Jack."

"But the police cleared both of them. They even got a warrant to search the house, came up with zilch."

"But one of them is an abuser. There's the proof."

"Hardly. Pure inference. Not even a name. There's no provenance on the file, and the victim is dead."

"And we are dead in the water again, Counselor.

"Prosecutor."

"One more entry to read. The penultimate one."

> i had almost forgotten about this file. 2 2 long. i met someone. he is awesome. so smart. helping me escape. i can do it. with him. i found his pix. getting used 2 it. he's old. i dont care. beautiful. beautiful mind. no russell crowe. but. we met last weekend. met 4 real. i want him. first time. i want him. impossible. i am just a geeky girl. someone 2 help with math. nex time maybe. impossible.

Brad's face was reddening as they read to themselves. He cleared his throat, breaking the silence. "Well, we're still clueless."

thirty-three

BRAD STARED AT the transcript. "It's gotta be right here, right in front of us. This is it, all we got. If we accept that this was not fabricated, then it is an authentic record of a real exchange between Reggi and her killer. Except it was not me. That"—he jabbed at the paper—"is not me." He leaned closer. "No, it is not me. It was right there in front of us all this time. Here, look at that line."

She read it aloud.

TUTOR-10: Came back early. We need to meet.

"But look at the handle."

"Okay, it says 'TUTOR-10', and that is you."

"No, it is not me. I'm TUTOR-10. This message came from T-U-T-ZERO-R-DASH-ONE-ZERO. See? It's expectation bias. We expected it to be TUTOR-10, so that's how we read it. All of us. Even the police forensics people." He jumped up from his chair. "This only looks like a dialogue with me, from my account, but it's from a completely different account."

"And there would be an administrative entry for the account, when whoever it was registered as a tutor."

"No, don't you see, those applications are processed by hand. They never would have allowed that handle. It had to be a student, and students can only register from inside their school, remember."

"And something else." Gillian was now tapping her foot, agitated. "The student had to know Regina and know about her . . . about you and her."

"We just need to find out who registered that handle."

Gillian was already firing up her laptop. "You know the login credentials for WesLee. Here, you do it."

"Right." He worked his way from the home page to the FAQ page where he clicked on a tiny yellow dot that had been planted by GeekGirl13. He typed the login command he had been given, but the screen stayed the same. He tried again with the same results. "Let me try my laptop. Maybe it only works from my machine." It didn't. "The backdoor has been closed and locked. I'm going to have to call Phoebe."

Brad raised GeekGirl13 through MoomBeam and told her what was happening.

"Chill, Bradster. Let me do some checking. Stay logged in on MoomBeam. I'll beam you back when I have something."

Brad and Gillian stared at the screen until the ringtone came ten minutes later.

"Not good, Bradster. They found the backdoor and bricked it up. They've got some new software that I don't know how to defeat. Not yet. I put out word to some other hackers, but it could take time before anything useful comes back."

"I need to get back in. Now."

"Why?"

"We think we know who the killer might be. We need to check who is registered to a particular InStarTute handle. It had to be a student who knew Reggi."

"You don't need to break into WesLee for that. There's a duplicate registry at each school for its own students. We just search the school computer systems. Shit, a six-year-old script kiddie can do that."

"There's what, 400 some high schools in the Commonwealth? How long will that take?"

"Not too long, there's only 392. I can code up a bot that will crawl all the high schools systems looking for the record. But why don't we start with Ipswich? What's the handle you are looking for?"

"I'll spell it out: T, U, T, digit zero, R, dash, digit one, digit zero. Uppercase letters."

"Got it. Oh, I see! And now, in through our special gateway, and over to the InStarTute local list, and . . . down, down, down . . . Here it is. Hey, I know this kid."

"Who is it? Who's the kid?"

"His name is Aaron Pretzky. He sometimes hangs with Reggi's stepbrother. You think?"

"Listen, Phoebe, you must not say anything about this to anyone. Not a word. Okay?"

"Yeah. Sure. But you think?"

"Maybe, but this is going to take some more work. I'll keep you in the loop, but keep it quiet."

Phoebe disconnected and Brad reached for his cellphone.

"What are you going to do?"

"Well, I thought I would call someone I know with the state police, but, now that I think about it, I'm going to call someone nearer to home." He dialed.

"Lieutenant Lefkowitz, please. Sure, I'll hold. Tell him it's Bradley Williams."

There was a long pause, then an impatient voice. "Lefkowitz here. What's up, Mr. Williams?"

"Do you have ready access to the Bellingham case files? Like that incriminating chat transcript?"

"Yeah, I can get it."

"Then do, I'll wait."

"You tell me what this is about before I go pawing through files?"

"You'll see. Just get the transcript."

Several minutes passed before the Lieutenant picked up the phone again. "Okay. Got it. Now what is this about?"

"What's the handle of the person the girl was chatting with?"

"TUTOR-10."

"No, read it more carefully, one letter at a time, look closely."

"All right, I'll play. T, U, T, . . . Holy shit! It's a zero not an oh. That would be a different ID, wouldn't it?"

"Yes, and if you get a search warrant for the student user registry from the InStarTute website, you will find out which high school student created that deliberately deceptive handle and used it to lure Regina Bellingham to her death."

"You already know, don't you."

"Yeah, but you need to do your own work so the evidence is clean. Get your warrant, then get your kid."

"Mr. Williams?"

"Yeah."

"Thanks. Thanks for the tip, for setting us straight. I'm glad it all worked out for you."

"Me, too. Me, too." He thumbed the cellphone off.

◊

The rhythms of his life were lost, the drum beats that once centered and stabilized Brad had segued into the cymbal crashes of crises and were drowned out by the parade of events that had marched in. By the time his mother died after a blessedly brief battle with pneumonia, Brad's equilibrium was completely gone. He acted as a responsible robot through the arrangements and the funeral—right up until the moment he stood over her casket.

"She was beautiful. Is." His body shook as he fought for composure. "I love you, Mom." He sniffled as the sluice opened and the tears flooded out: tears for her, tears for Reggi, and tears for himself. Gillian held him for long minutes as the few of his mother's friends in the room gave them space.

Back at Gillian's, he collapsed into disorderly depression, beaten down by the losses. With his detective work done and without outside demands, Brad wandered around the house without aim or purpose for several days. Then he threw a mental switch and slowly began constructing a fresh cadence to counter his lethargy and contain his inattention. Mornings began with orange juice on the deck with Gillian and a copy of the *Wall Street Journal*, then a long hike on the trail through the woods that started and finished at Pale Pond. Afternoons he spent reading journal articles online followed by a desultory pass at the draft of a memoir on which he pretended to work seriously. Then Gillian would return from her office to distract him for the evening.

The call came in on his cellphone one mid-morning as he approached Pale Pond.

"It's Lefkowitz here. I shouldn't tell you this, but I wanted to bring you up to date. We picked him up. You were right, but you got the wrong kid."

"What do you mean?"

"Pretzky was along for the ride. He helped with the online trickery, but he didn't do it. He's going to plead out on a lesser charge in exchange for testimony."

"Testimony?"

"Against Jack Bellingham."

"Which one? Which Jack Bellingham?"

"Junior."

"What happened? What really happened?"

"Look, I don't want to queer the whole deal. You understand, we didn't even have this conversation, but I figured you would want to know. That's all I can tell you now."

◊

Gillian pulled into the driveway and squealed to a stop. She ran into the house and found Brad in the home office, staring at his laptop screen. "Did you see *The Globe*?"

"Not yet. What's the story?"

"You sure you want to hear this?"

"Yeah. I'm sure." He added a period to the sentence he was typing, saved off the copy of his memoir, and turned his full attention to Gillian, who bounced with impatience.

"Okay. So the DA gets two-for-one without a trial. Our boy Pretzky spills everything and is ready to testify. His lawyer bargains down from rape and accessory to murder to indecent assault on a minor under the age of eighteen. He'll do five-to-ten, then spend the rest of his life on the Sexual Offenders Registry. Jack folds and confesses over the advice of his attorney. He's going away for life."

"That's the box score, a shutout, but do we know the real story?"

"Yes. Jack was jealous of you, because you were getting something and he was not, not any longer. He got this numbskull idea to pretend to be you to lure her where he could force her and get his piece of the action. He conspired with the Pretzky kid to set up the fake account and to lend a hand. He and Pretzky forced her into the pickup in Springfield, then drove to a deserted stretch of a fire trail: just a random place marked on a map. They started to rape her in the back of the pickup, but she got away before it was Jack's turn. He was furious. She was running barefoot in the dark wearing only her torn blouse. She tripped and hit her head. Jack caught up with her but she fought. He banged her head against a rock until she stopped struggling. Then he raped her. She was already dead. The boys panicked. They used Big Jack's tools to dig a shallow grave, then used the drain cleaner from the back of the pickup truck to try to destroy the evidence.

"For a couple of losers they did pretty well—more luck than skill. The drain cleaner worked even better than they could have expected, and they took her remaining clothes back to Ipswich, put them through the laundry a few times, then folded and hung them back in Regina's room. They missed the pen in the dark, the only thing that really seemed to implicate you."

"It did, in actual fact. I was the one who let her keep it. It was simple dumb luck that they didn't have a print good enough to match. Anyway, those two almost got away with it. I almost ended up doing their time for them. Good thing I met you."

"Good thing for both of us." She put her arms around him, squeezing, holding onto him as tightly as she could manage.

thirty-four

BRAD PUT DOWN THE BASKET of laundry and started folding the load of tee-shirts. "Armand says he can get me back tutoring on the website. The application and review is a joke, anyway. So, I'll be able to start contributing around here."

"You are contributing. You do most of the cooking and all of the laundry, and you keep the lady of the house contented."

He added another folded shirt to the stack. "I meant contribute, for real. You're a lawyer. What am I?"

"You're a mathematician. Still. And keeping me contented isn't real? You sure you don't want to rephrase that?"

"You know what I mean. All that stuff doesn't add up to what you do. I feel like a kept man."

"Exactly. Those are my intentions: to keep you. You do plenty to earn your keep."

"Yeah, like spending half my days on math mumblings and the other half brooding over maps. Laundry is not enough to keep me occupied for more than a few hours a week."

"I expect you to mumble over math, darling—like I said, you're a mathematician—but what is this about maps?"

"Reggi's map. There were three things in her little encrypted

231

treasure box: her diary, a headshot of me, and that satellite view of somewhere. The time stamp on the file means it was saved off during the first year after her mother abandoned her. It means something. I've been trying to find a fit to somewhere on the planet. It's hopeless."

"Why don't you just match it, search GoogleMaps for a match?"

"I've been trying to do something like that, even writing a little program, but that won't work. The online maps are constantly being improved and updated, new aerial photos and satellite photos taken, so you could be looking at the exact same spot and a program, even a smart program, wouldn't see a match. No, it has to be done by hand, and that could take centuries."

"Do we have any other clues? Anything?"

"The title of the file, pickupx.jpg, whatever that means."

"Maybe there's something in her diary, maybe an entry around the same time."

"Well, that we can check. Let me finish folding and I'll meet you in the office."

◊

When they retrieved the Tumi.docx diary, they found one of the widely spaced entries was dated a few days before the aerial shot.

> he was away again, the pickup pioneer. more power line work, western mass. it's a relief when he's away. i also get this dread. maybe because last time was about a year ago right around my b'day. just before mom disappears.

"Pickup, his pickup. What do you think, Brad? Does it make the search more doable if we narrow it to Western Massachusetts?"

"Maybe. The photo is mostly wooded, some winding dirt roads, maybe rolling hills, what looks to be a power line cutting across the corner. Could be a lot of places. Just Berkshire county alone has gotta be close to a thousand square miles."

"I used to be pretty good with jigsaw puzzles. Maybe I could help. If we had a big printout of the whole area, satellite view, blown up, like a real map, maybe we could spot something that looks like that one piece of the territory."

"I don't know about one big picture, but we could match the scale by zooming in on GoogleMaps until the trees look about the same size as in the photo. Then we could slowly scan over the whole county. Might cut the search time down to mere weeks or months instead of years."

"Bet you I can find it in a few days."

"Bet you can't."

Brad worked on tweaking the zoom on GoogleMaps, then they started in the northwest corner of the state, at the border with New York and Vermont, inching their way onscreen across the county, glancing back and forth between the browser and the printed copy of Regina's map, then bumping the view south a notch for the next scan east-to-west. After a couple of back-and-forth sweeps, Brad lost interest and patience, but Gillian persisted. He was asleep in the extra chair when he heard the shout. "Eureka!"

thirty-five

THE TWO OF THEM CHECKED the GPS coordinates on Gillian's smart-phone, then started hiking up the rutted fire trail. All of a sudden Brad stopped. "I know where we are. This is near where they found Reggi, where she was killed. Look, there's where the power line cuts through. It's over that way, over that rise. This is just too weird."

"Are you sure? What are you talking about? You couldn't have been here. Unless . . . no."

"There were the aerial news photos and the crime scene photos at the trial. It just all seems familiar. If we cross over that rise, we'll be right there."

"If that's true, you are suggesting that the girl knew the spot where she was going to be killed years before she was killed. That's creepy." She looked down at the topo map they had marked with the coordinates coinciding with the indicated spot from the aerial photo. "It's not the same. The spot on the map is over that way." She pointed. "It's just some kind of coincidence."

"It's not coincidence. Reggi had reason to be interested in this spot. She sought out this particular area out here in the Berkshires and took a screen shot of it from GoogleMaps. She saved it and named the file pickupx.jpg for a reason. She's leading us here."

"Brad, don't you start going all mystical on me."

"I'm not. That's not the way I meant. I meant metaphorically." His words came in short bursts as the fire road took a turn west and the climb steepened. "There."

Where he pointed, a simple wood-plank shed stood, barely more than a lean-to and just big enough to stand up in. It had once been locked, but a rusty hasp, padlock still closed, now dangled from a single bolt on the splintered door. Brad tugged at the door and the rotten wood around its hinges gave way.

Gillian looked up from her smartphone. "This is it, all right, the exact coordinates. What is it? Anything in it?"

"Nothing. It was maybe a temporary toolshed, maybe from when they were running the power line, maybe some other construction project. It's empty now. Anything left here has long since sprouted legs." He stepped inside. The dank smell of earth and rotting wood filled the air. He looked around, straining to see in the shadows. "Oh."

"What?"

"Oh no, no."

"What is it?"

"She was here. Here in this shed."

"What are you talking about? How do you know?"

"Look, inside the door, just around the corner." Gillian took a step inside and turned. There was just room for the two of them. "I don't see anything."

"There, hanging from that nail."

"I still don't . . . oh. It looks like earbuds."

"Skullcandy. Cobalt blue and purple. Very uncommon. Reggi had a pair. Only ones I ever saw like that. She was very proud of them. Swag from her thirteenth birthday."

"How? How did they get here? This is just getting weird again, too weird."

"She had them the last time I saw her, that's all I know. She must have tried to take shelter here the night she was killed. They snagged on the nail. Or she hung them there. In the dark, in a scuffle, who would have noticed?"

"What about the police? Surely they searched this whole area."

"What time of day? You almost missed them and there's a sliver of sunlight through the roof almost spotlighting them."

"I still don't get how she could have ended up at this place on the map that she predicted."

"We're stuck on prediction. There's another explanation, a simpler one. Something led her to mark the location of this shed on the screenshot, and something led Jack and his buddy to turn onto this particular obscure trail that put them near here. It had to be the same something, but I sure don't know what it is."

He reached for the earbuds. She stopped him. "If you are right, this is a crime scene. That's evidence. We need to tell the police."

"The case is closed. The killers are already in jail. What could this matter?"

"Leave it." In the shaft of light stabbing through a break in the roof, Gillian's expression was forceful. Brad shook his head in resignation, then stepped aside to let her exit first.

Deep in thought, he walked slowly away from the shed, toward a granite outcropping. He sat, staring down-slope, shifting his gaze from side-to-side. He unfolded the printout of the satellite shot, then resurveyed his surroundings.

Gillian approached, clearly getting impatient. "We need to let the police know about the shed. There could still be useful evidence to be recovered."

"Useful? For what? Prosecuting raccoons? Jack confessed. It's over." His frown of concentration deepened. "You have a signal on your smartphone?"

"I think, but we don't have to call it in now."

"I don't want to make a call; I want to go to GoogleMaps. There's something on the screenshot that I want to check out. That spot, there." She dug into her backpack and handed the phone to him. She watched over his shoulder as he zoomed in repeatedly then backed off a step, twisted the phone at an angle, slid the image over slightly, and zoomed back in.

"This satellite image is at least a year-and-a-half old, maybe older. I don't imagine they refresh the images over empty areas like this all that frequently. It was late fall or winter. See, the trees are bare, but there's no snow cover. Here, this light streak," he pointed, "is the ledge I am sitting on. And over here," he slid the image over slightly, "is something on the image. But if you look in that direction, downhill, where the ground levels off some, there's nothing." He held the phone up as if to take a tilted photo. "See? Now you see it, now you don't. Or then you see it, and now . . ."

"It's grown over. So what? It's early fall, that was winter."

"And that spot was cleared, freshly cleared. See on the satellite image how it's a slightly different color than the area around it. Why would there have been this roughly rectangular, cleared area in the scrub? Let's go down and take a look."

He led the way down, angling far to the right to avoid some of the thickest brush, then doubling back. "It should be right about here." He took a few more steps and his foot sunk ankle-deep into a thick layer of leaves and needles. "Yes, right here. Help me brush aside the duff." He bent down and started scooping out the debris.

Gillian knelt and started brushing the damp covering to the side. "I found something," she said, holding up an oblong, dirt-covered stick.

"A stick."

"No," she said, brushing off dirt and debris, "a bone."

"Animals."

"Animals may have been here, but . . . No, I am no anatomist, but

I'll wager this is a human bone."

"Let me see. Hmmm." He held the bone next to the side of his boot. "Maybe. About the right size for a metatarsus." He dug some more with his hands through the loose soil where Gillian had found the bone. His hand closed around something fatter and longer. "Tibia, maybe. If we keep digging, we will probably find a lot more."

"No, we're not going to keep digging; just leave it. Human remains have to be reported. We really do have to tell the police."

"Yes, we do, although how we do it is still open to negotiation. You realize that we are only a few hundred yards from where they found the body. Just dumb luck they found her, found Regina, and not this one. Just dumb luck they stopped on the other side of the ridge and didn't thoroughly check out the shack. Why should they? They had what they were looking for. But I am guessing it is not dumb luck that there were two people buried so close together out here."

"Well, we'll find out once the police identify the body."

"If they do. It's been years, probably."

"Well, let's go back into town and report it so they can get started." Brad shook his head and Gillian raised her eyebrows. "What? Is there more? Brad, talk to me."

"When will you ever start trusting and believing in me?"

"I do. Mostly. It's just that there have been so many . . . surprises since I met you, and I am just perpetually on alert. I'm sorry. But why can't we just go to the police?"

"Because my life is beginning to settle down again. Because people still stare, but they no longer cross to the other side of the street when I approach. Because the recent Coconut Club meetings have had more than just you, me, and Armand. That's why. I don't want to be in the papers again. So, let's just send an anonymous tip to the state police. Okay?"

"Okay. Let's go. It's getting chilly."

◊

Brad's heart jumped when he answered the doorbell. It was Detective Sergeant Hamilton.

"Can I come in?"

"Gillian's not here. She's still at the office. I'm . . . I'm just hanging out, waiting for her to—"

"It's okay. Everyone in town knows about you two. No big deal. And we know you sent the anonymous tip about the other body."

"What tip?"

"Hey, play it anyway you like, Williams. We may be small town cops but we aren't dumb cops. It was a no brainer figuring it out. You and your lawyer friend were spotted on your way up the fire road. We keep our eyes open out here, keep our eyes on people. That's how this kind of town works."

"Will they ever stop? Will they . . . ?" Brad choked off his words before his voice rose too far.

"Forget? Will they ever forget? Is that what you want to know? Well, even small towns have an imperfect memory. In another generation this whole business will be a local legend, with most of the details scrambled and the names forgotten. But it takes time. People don't know whether they can trust you; they don't know what to believe. You're an outsider. So is Gillian. Give it time. By the time your kids are graduating from the Regional High School, you and your family will be neighbors."

"Lot of assumptions in there, Sergeant."

"Hey, it's what we do best. It's what makes up small town police work. And small town life. But I didn't come here as the Welcome Wagon. I thought you might want to know about the murder, the body. We've identified it."

"Already? I thought the forensics might take forever."

The Sergeant laughed and started coughing. "Forensics? We had the identity before the County Coroner had finished exhuming the body. The dumbass perp buried the body along with the victim's wallet. Real leather, rotted to nothing, but not her driver's license. I understand those things take five-hundred years to decompose. Talia Josephson Bellingham, the girl's mother. They've already picked up and charged the stepfather."

"The stepfather? Not the brother?"

"Not the brother. We questioned him right away, of course, but he denied it. Absolutely convinced that the stepmother had run away, abandoned the family. And he had nothing to lose by confessing, really. He's already doing life without parole. No, the dumbass dad tried to pin it on his own son when we brought him in for questioning. Some father."

"Then how do you know it was him?"

"Straight out of the detective stories, something that never happens for real. He says, 'I didn't stab her.' Can you believe that? We didn't even have the autopsy report yet, but there was a butcher knife with the body. The idiot must have panicked and thrown everything into the grave. The knife matched the set at his house, the one with a butcher knife with a mismatched handle. There was even a bit of pencil scribble on a map in the glove box of his pickup, marking the location of some tool shed right nearby. Must have been from a job he had worked on.

"Anyway, if the guy is smart, he'll just confess and save the Commonwealth a lot of trouble. But, probably not, since he seems only to be just smart enough to have gotten himself a headline-chasing lawyer."

part four: corollary

thirty-six

"THAT'S THE LAST." Brad slid the overflowing cardboard carton onto the granite breakfast bar.

Gillian laughed. "For a bachelor who lived alone in a tiny apartment, you sure managed to accumulate a lot of junk in the time since you moved back in."

"Stuff. Not junk. I threw out the junk, three trash bags worth."

"What are we going to do with all this . . . this stuff?" She tugged at a cord that dangled from the box just deposited by Brad. The cable popped free and a silver ball dangling from the end started swinging. "What on earth is this?"

"Now? It's a pendulum. But it was once a webcam. I was going to extract the camera chip from it and—"

"And throw it in the trash. Right?" She, dangled it over the white plastic bin in the corner.

"Yeah, that's right. That's what I was going to do with it. And the rest of this—"

"Junk!"

"—stuff, I was going to stash temporarily in the garage."

"Until the weekend, when you can sort it into two piles, one of which you will throw in the trash and the other of which you will box up and throw in the trash."

"Such a harsh landlady you are."

"Lover. Harsh lover I are. Am."

"So, it's official. We're lovers and I am moved in. Lease at the apartment terminated, Rubicon crossed."

"Finally. Took our time, didn't we."

"And who was it who all this time was worried about giving up her privacy, her freedom, her house?"

"I was just concerned about how you would fit in here, important details. Once you started doing laundry and promised to cook, everything fell into place. Now I know where you fit in: the servants' quarters, obviously."

"Would that be the same as the master bedroom, ma'am?"

"See? Already you are calling me 'ma'am,' just as I predicted so long ago. If that's the way it's going to be, I'll expect dinner at seven sharp."

"As you wish."

"Very good, Farm Boy."

◊

Dinner was simple. For the occasion of the official move, Gillian opened a superior Chianti Reserva from her modest collection, and Brad replicated as best he could the frittata from the first meal he had cooked for her.

Gillian pushed back her plate with a contented smile on her lips. "Oh, I forgot to mention it. I heard today that the old man plea-bargained down to second degree murder. He might make parole before he dies."

"Why would the DA do that? They had him."

"Murder trials are expensive, a long time has passed, and they didn't want to risk that he might walk. That's how the law works outside of law school. In a way, it's justice, I suppose. It wasn't part of a premeditated assault like with Jack, Jr. The father acted impulsively. He was desperate to stop the mother from going to the police after she caught him with her daughter."

"So, Regina and her mother are both dead, and both the stepfather and stepbrother are in jail. The whole family. Nobody left."

"Well, we don't know about Regina's father."

"Yeah, I do still wonder who her father was. A pity they wouldn't release a full copy of the birth certificate."

"We at least know his last name."

"We do? How? I thought the name had been redacted."

"It was, but it was also right in front of us, just like that online handle. A couple of years after Regina was born, her mother petitioned for a name change and took on the father's surname. Apparently, she was never happy with her own parents' name. She was adopted. In Israel. According to her petition, she claimed to have been stolen at birth from her biological mother, a Yemini immigrant to Israel. I guess it happened; there are stories, anyway. So, it turns out Regina's father was named Josephson. The mother would have been a grad student at Boston University at the time she got pregnant."

"BU? Josephson? Not Arnon Josephson, the mathematician? Yes, of course. Makes sense. He's brilliant. Never made a big splash in mathematics, but his name is on a lot of solid papers. His Erdös number is three."

"What? Air-dish number?"

"Erdös, Hungarian. It's a sort of game among mathematicians, like Six Degrees of Kevin Bacon. Paul Erdös was prolific; he published more papers than any other mathematician in history. Your Erdös number is how many co-authored papers you have to jump to get to one written with Erdös. If you wrote one with him, your Erdös number is one; my number is seven. Anyway, Josephson did a lot of original work. If he is Regina's father that explains a lot."

"The apple doesn't fall far from Newton's tree, I suppose."

"No, and I have an idea. What would you think of a drive to Boston this weekend?"

"What I would think? I would think that you would do almost anything to avoid having to sort out your junk in the garage."

◊

Over the phone, Professor Josephson was reluctant to meet with them, particularly when Brad told them they had something for him from his daughter.

"I have three grown sons," he said. "I think you have the wrong Professor Josephson."

"No, I don't think so. To the best of my knowledge, you never met your daughter, but you knew her mother well enough. Does the name Talia Diamond mean anything? She was a grad student at BU some seventeen, eighteen years ago. A non-traditional student, older, immigrant from Israel. Remember?"

There was no answer.

"Listen, sir, I am not trying to pull anything on you. I just have some things from your daughter that you might want to have. She was a mathematician, like you."

"My daughter? A mathematician? What was her name?"

"Regina. Regina Elizabeth Josephson Bellingham on her Ipswich High School records."

"That girl, in the papers, the one who was molested by some predator, right?"

Brad ground his teeth. "No, that's the girl, but she was molested and killed by her stepbrother. So, can we see you?"

"What a sordid business, that. Look, I'll meet you in my office on campus. Saturday at two. I can . . . come in to consult with some students. I don't want my family involved in this. It was a long time ago. I was only an Associate Professor then. You understand."

"Oh yes."

"Two, then, Saturday. You can find my office? The building's on Cummington Mall. I'm on the first floor, just down the hall from the Department Chair."

"I'm sure we can find you."

◊

The meeting started awkwardly. Brad gave Josephson a marked-up printout of Regina's thesis, which the professor flipped through without much interest as they talked.

"I was young," he said. "Rachel and I—my first wife—were struggling. Talia was very bright, very eager to learn. She spent a lot of time in my office. Weekends, mostly. She worked, if I remember correctly. She told me about being pregnant, of course, at the end of the term. I gave her some money to take care of it and to help her out. That was it. I never saw her again. She must have dropped out of school. She was in her mid-twenties, I think, a whole life ahead of her. I didn't want to see her tied down with a kid. Do you know what happened with her?"

"Yes, after she had the baby she worked odd jobs to make ends meet. She eventually married a construction worker who molested her daughter and murdered Talia after she caught him. That was her life. And that," he tapped the paper on Josephson's desk, "is what remains: the summation of her life, the summation of her daughter's life—your daughter's life. Read it. I think you might find it interesting."

Josephson looked down. "The title is rather unexpected. Odd. 'A Concise Manual Proof of the Four-Color Theorem.' That hardly seems possible. A high-school girl, you say?"

"A brilliant high-school girl. She especially liked topology and graph theory, was learning your field, computational complexity. She was using the reworking of the Four-Color Theorem as a warm-up exercise. Her target was the Millennium Prize, one of the few routes to real money in modern mathematics. She saw it as her escape pod. She originally had some ideas for the Poincaré Conjecture, but then Perelman beat her to the solution. She was furious when he turned down the million dollars. She was considering attacking P versus NP, but this draft of a new proof of the Four-Color Theorem is as far as she got in her career."

"She would have been in grade school when Perelman was awarded the prize for the Poincaré proof."

"Middle school. She skipped ahead. I told you, she was smart."

Josephson stared at the stapled paper on his desk as though it had suddenly metamorphosed from something else. "Yes. I'll read it. Is there anything else I can do for you?"

"No, not for me. You can't do anything, and you can't undo anything. Maybe you can do something with the paper. It's a little above my head, some of it. I'm smart enough, and I've taught college-level math, but I wasn't in your daughter's league." His voice started to choke. "My ... my wife is waiting outside. We have a long drive back."

"Where do you live?"

"West Hopeland."

"And that is where?"

"Western Mass."

"Oh, right. Now it comes back to me. The trial and all."

"And all." Brad stood and held out his hand. There was a heartbeat of hesitation before it was accepted.

"My daughter, she was your student?"

"Yes, my student." And more, he was thinking, so much more, something you might even know about.

The professor's face softened noticeably. "What was she like?"

"A lot like her mother, I would imagine. Petite, quick-witted, impatient. Generous. Trusting but guarded at the same time." He stopped himself from letting the line of thought continue. "She loved music almost as much as math, but not the adolescent crazes of the day—no, for her it was Tears for Fears, Phil Collins, Denton Reynolds, what she called old stuff."

Josephson blinked hard. "I see. I will read this, I will. Do have a safe drive home, Mr. Williams."

"And you have a good read, Professor Josephson." Brad turned and strode out the door before anything more could be said.

◊

With a stop at a rest area on the Mass Pike for coffee and French fries, it was well after dark when Gillian pulled off Silver Point Road and up the steep drive. A strained silence had settled over them on the last miles, as if they were returning from a funeral. Before Brad could get out to open the garage door, Gillian reached over and took his hand.

"You gave him the paper, didn't you, the last thing you had from her."

"I gave him the hardcopy with my notes on it, yes. But there's the original PDF file somewhere on my laptop. Funny, in this day and age, it is hard to say what original means. Her work was original, but the paper is just paper. The work is," he looked through the sunroof toward stars he couldn't see, "out there. Ideas. Ideas have no mass, only velocity. Like light, I guess.

"Sorry for that. Endings punch my profoundness buttons. But the paper wasn't the last thing I have of her, from her."

Gillian gave him an "oh-really" look that reminded him of how quickly her curiosity could turn into anxiety. He reached into the breast pocket of his sports jacket and held up a small plastic bag. "She left me something. Remember?"

"What is it? I can't really tell in this light."

"Earbuds, hers. I couldn't leave them at the shed only to end up in some evidence locker. I've kept them with me ever since. She would have wanted me to have them. She once said that at thirty-six, it was about time I owned a pair of earbuds. She could not understand how anyone could listen to music without cords draping from their ears. Do you think I should try them?"

"I do. I think she was right. It's about time you learned how to listen to music while properly plugged in."

thirty-seven

BRISK, EARLY AUTUMN BREEZES were shaking the yellowing leaves of the birch stand at the corner of the yard as Brad headed back up the drive, shuffling the stack of mail as he walked. Amidst the junk mail and catalogs was a hand-addressed padded mailer with a Boston return address. He moved it to the top of the stack and, inside, set the pile on the breakfast bar.

Gillian called out, "Did you bring in the mail, Darling?"

"Yes, Darling, that's what I said I was doing."

"Oh, I couldn't hear you. I was down in my office. Still researching. Adoptions are so complicated these days." She smiled broadly as she crossed the room, and the irritation drained from Brad as he noticed the crinkles at the corners of her eyes and remembered once again why he had fallen in love with her. "Any mail from Angie?" she asked.

"No, and I don't expect any either. Neither of us was ever much of a letter writer, but I suspect she'll start Skyping again once she's settled in at the University. Funny how that works. I only just get my daughter back, and I lose her again, off to college. Too bad she had to wait until she was eighteen to be able to see me again.

"Timing. My life is outlined in misplaced moments. I wish Mom could have lived to see her granddaughter off to college. In a way, the pneumonia was a blessing, a step off the down escalator my mother was riding. But she would have liked the young adult that Angie has become."

"I really like her. I do. I am so glad she could visit for a few days before driving out to Chicago. Watching you two . . . you make quite a pair. The banter and the affectionate teasing never stop, do they?"

"No, I guess not. But we can get serious, too. We had a couple of real dad-and-daughter talks while she was here. Life, love, learn-ing—grand schemes and abandoned dreams." Brad's eyes roamed the kitchen, pausing, then moving on with his thoughts. "Can't get over how she's grown. The last time we were in the same room together she was, like, sixteen, in court. Now . . ."

"Does she know the whole story? I mean, about Regina."

"She does. We talked about it."

"And? What's her take on it?"

"I assume by 'it' you mean the affair, not the work on some ob-scure mathematics."

"Is that what it is, now? Is that how you see it looking back? An affair?"

"I really don't know what word . . . what words . . . It was some-thing that happened, that changes with distance. I said at the time that I loved her, and I suppose that was true then, but my experi-ence of love is already so different now, only a couple of years later. Maybe I'm growing up. Maybe that changes the semantics."

There was a long silence as Gillian rounded the breakfast bar and chose one of the stools beside Brad. "Maybe it does. You know, I just put something together for myself. I had this crush on my biology teacher when I was sixteen. Mr. Atwood was new, fresh out of grad school and matinee-idol handsome, with a Cary Grant moustache and thick, curly hair. He'd been in the air force for some time, so he might have been early thirties. If he had made the moves, I would have gladly surrendered my virginity to him, but he was recently married—the bastard—and oblivious to my clumsy flirtations. Or smart enough to ignore them.

"I said crush. That's what I call it now, but then it was love. I was head-over-heels in love with him at sixteen; at fifty I re-label it, dismiss it as a passing preoccupation, but then it was real. The fact that experiences look different looking back does not mean they were nothing at the time. Or unimportant."

"Well said. Worthy of the Coconut Club."

"Sincerely said. Maybe I am starting to understand. Not approve, mind you."

"I don't want or expect your approval, but forgiveness might be nice."

"I'm not even sure you need forgiveness. Maybe from yourself."

"Angie said something like that, too. She said that she could understand, given Reggi's background—the abuse and all—how it would make it hard for her to make good choices about men, how she might be drawn to someone also older—but gentler, safer." He scratched at his forehead. "Angie has a somewhat different take on me, on my role." He chuckled. "She is not ready to condemn me as a defiler of young girls—I am her beloved father, after all—but she is not exactly accepting either.

"She said I was always a bit immature, emotionally young for my age, like a part of me never got much beyond sixteen, someone with little sense of perspective and not enough appreciation of consequences. She was kinda, well, brutal in some ways. But she also said she felt as if it were in some way her fault, that the whole dust-up with her false accusations somehow planted the seeds for what happened later with Regina. I suppose she may never completely forgive herself either. "

"Your whole family is always ready to take on the blame."

"Yeah, I guess. You know what else she said? She said what I really needed was a strong older woman. Someone like you. She likes you. She thinks we're a good match."

"Me, too." She gave him a peck on the cheek. "So, no letter from Angie. Anything interesting in the mail?"

Brad reached behind himself and grabbed the padded envelope from the top of the stack. "Just this. Addressed to Dr. and Mrs. Bradley Williams. Presumptuous, wouldn't you say?"

"Or merely premature." She grinned even more broadly.

"Does this mean you might finally say yes and agree to marry me?"

"Maybe. Does that mean you will finally go back to graduate school and finish your doctorate?"

"Maybe. But, first, let's see what is in our presumptuous packet?"

He tore open the mailer and extracted a bound journal: *Complexities: The Journal of the Academy of Metasystems and Computational Analysis.* A folded, stapled paper peeked from inside. He slid it out and started reading.

Dear Dr. and Mrs. Bradley Williams,

I know it has been a long time since our brief meeting. I do apologize for any offence I might have caused with my behavior on that occasion. It was a most awkward encounter; I am sure for you as well. I was completely taken aback by your disclosures, as I would imagine you can understand.

I read through the paper on the Four-Color Theorem even before I left my office at the University that day. Regina must have been a truly remarkable girl. The paper bore the hallmarks of a gifted if undisciplined mind. I could see from the marginalia and annotations that your own contributions were not inconsiderable. If I recall, you minimized your role when we met, but I think you underestimate what you brought to the collaboration, to the relationship.

At any rate, I studied the paper with great care and continued to be impressed with its brilliance and originality of method. Unfortunately, it was also wrong. The proof was flawed. It was a dead-end line of reasoning. The irreparable errors in the argument begin on page 32 and continue through 36, as can be seen from my notes on the attached photocopies.

That said, I was rather taken by the hubris of the so-called canonical reduction theory, which seemed to hold promise as a novel tool of analysis in computational complexity. I presented an outline of it at a faculty seminar here, which stirred the interest of my doctoral student, Bridget Steenhausen. Bridget and I have since worked closely on the theory, and the fruits of that collaboration can be seen in the accompanying journal article. As you will note, I have credited your role in the Acknowledgements section at the end. I hope that I can be forgiven the small liberty taken with surnames in the authorship.

Yours truly,

Arnon Josephson
Alexander Kline Professor of Mathematics and Computer Science
Boston University

Brad opened the journal and paged through it. "Here it is. 'Canonical Reduction Theory as a Method of Simplifying Classifications for Complex, Heterogeneous Collections.'" Brad started to cry. "It lists the authors as Bridget M. Steenhausen, Ph.D. (Cand.), Arnon T. Josephson, Ph.D., and Regina E. Josephson.

"She made it into print." He laughed as the tears streamed down his face. "You realize, this means her Erdös number is four. Beats mine."

He handed the open journal to Gillian. "Here, read the epigraph. I can't . . . can't manage right now." He closed his eyes and listened.

Gillian read in silence, and then out loud, her voice barely above a whisper. "'Teach, that you may learn again, and learn that you might teach me.' Denton Reynolds. And there's a dedication just below: *In memoriam, Regina Elizabeth Josephson, 1996-2013.*"

appendix

"Teachable Moments"

DENTON REYNOLDS (1959-1997), a New England singer-songwriter best known for the song "Teachable Moments," was active in the Boston-Cambridge music scene from the late 1970s until the early 1990s. Born into a musical family in Portland, Maine, he was raised by his mother, a high school chorus teacher and founder of the counter-cultural Down East Consciousness Collective; his father, a jazz clarinetist, had abandoned the family shortly after Denton was born. Self-taught on the guitar after his older brother, Seth, discontinued the instrument, Denton started his first band, Portmanteau, at the age of sixteen. At eighteen, he and his sixteen-year-old girlfriend, Simone Packard, who played bass guitar in Portmanteau, left Portland for Cambridge, Massachusetts. There, Denton was arrested for transporting a minor across state lines, charges that were later dropped. He wrote "Teachable Moments" in 1978 while still crashing with friends in Somerville. Having arrived late on the folk-rock scene, he debuted the song as a busker working Harvard Square in Cambridge. It is dedicated to Simone.

He recorded only one known album, on the Dented Rain label, with "Teachable Moments" as the title cut. In the album notes, he credited Phil Ochs, Bob Dylan, and Paul Simon as his principle poetic inspirations. His musical reputation rests mainly on pirated cassette tapes and, later, MP3 copies and a YouTube video of him playing the song at Passim, the storied Cambridge coffee house. Although he never gained national recognition, he had a strong New England following, especially in Massachusetts. He disappeared from the local folk-rock scene during much of the 1990s but made a comeback appearance at the Berkshire Buskers Music Fest in 1996.

Boston Globe music critic Shel Greenlaw wrote of the occasion: "The festival opened with the return of local hero Denton Reynolds, whose barebones baritone was backed by the latest incarnation of the ever-morphing Portland band, Portmanteau. With the drone of his simple, pedal-point melodies and the Rorschach poetry of his metaphor-layered lyrics, Reynolds mesmerized the capacity crowd of dedicated local folk-rock fans and finished with the audience on their feet in a seven-minute chant of the chorus from his signature song, 'Teachable Moments'."

The following year, Denton was found dead in his Watertown apartment, an apparent suicide. Simone Packard resurfaced to claim that her daughter, Denita, born in 1982, was Denton's child and rightful heir, but Packard was unsuccessful in court. Rights to Denton's work remain with Dented Rain Music and are administered by his older brother, Seth, as literary executor. Rumors of unreleased tracks for a never-completed second album persist.

"Teachable Moments"

Words and music by Denton Reynolds. Used with permission of Dented Rain Music, Ltd., and Seth Reynolds.

When the teacher becomes the student
And the classroom is the hall,
Then the teachings of philosophy
Must be rewritten on the wall.

So the scholars must relearn the primer,
As the lessons of their youth grow dimmer.
Still the pupils spy a hopeful glimmer
Down dark corridors of insight.
(Down dark corridors of insight.)

(chorus)
Teach, that you may learn again,
And learn that you might teach me.
In the answers of your questioning,
May your someday wisdom reach me.
(repeat)

Once I knew my own direction,
And for fortune I was bound.
Then there was no place for divinity
Or distractions to be found.

But you taught me I was just a beginner
On a journey where no one is the winner,
And the lines to follow keep getting thinner
On the fading map of insight.
(On the fading map of insight.)

(chorus)
Teach, that you may learn again,
And learn that you might teach me.
In the answers of your questioning,
May your someday wisdom reach me.
(repeat)

The teachable moments hide unheeded
In the twisted turns of time.
And the stanzas spin to infinity
In rewoven words of rhyme.

So we read our bibles cover-to-cover
For the timeless truth we hope to recover
And quotations we recite to each other
In elusive lines of insight.
(In elusive lines of insight.)

(chorus)
Teach, that you may learn again,
And learn that you might teach me.
In the answers of your questioning,
May your someday wisdom reach me.
(repeat)

author's footnote

WITH ONE EXCEPTION, all the mathematical references and allusions in this story are authentic. However, in as much as my background is in computer science rather than mathematics per se, I am hoping that I have not too badly confused the concepts or misrepresented the real mathematics. The single intentional exception to authenticity is in canonical reduction theory, a fanciful fiction that does not exist. Yet.